A Shadow of Himself

BOOKS BY MICHAEL DELVING

A SHADOW OF HIMSELF
DIE LIKE A MAN
THE DEVIL FINDS WORK
SMILING THE BOY FELL DEAD

A Shadow of Himself

by Michael Delving

CHARLES SCRIBNER'S SONS   NEW YORK

This book is for
Nancy and Aidan Chambers

I owe a debt of gratitude for advice and special information to Linda and Christopher Davis, Maurice Graham, Tom Hudson, and Gerald Pollinger, and particularly to J. R. H. Yeoman and A. F. Holford-Walker of the Council for the Protection of Rural England.

J. W.

The tendency among Americans is to think of England as a cosy little country with about four giant strides between villages. It is as correct as many of our other fixed notions, such as that the good guy always wins and the Bunny Club is sexy. There I was with a flat tire and no tools, on a country road which looked as if it hadn't been traveled since 1869, and all around me stretched fields and woods without a sign of human life. A group of cows came and observed me, round-eyed, but none of them had a workable suggestion. For sheer cosiness I might have been in the middle of the Arizona desert.

Not for the first time, I began to wonder if coming over had been such a good idea. Not for the first time, I cursed the inefficiency of the English who among other things could rent you a car without proper equipment. My friend and partner, Dave Cannon, is a great Anglophile. He would have found something apologetic to say. As for me, drawing on my Cherokee background and my imperfect knowledge of the language of my people, all I said was "Shit!"

I kicked aimlessly at the tire, which grinned squashily at me. I got out my map. Bartonbury, the village I was heading for, was five miles away. Between it and me were two tiny dots marked Tenterton and Dimmit St. Mary's, no more than hamlets in which I doubted there would be gas stations. But the other way was Cheltenham, from which I'd just driven through six miles of farmland. It would be best to go forward. I locked the car and started off on foot.

9

I hadn't gone a hundred paces when I heard a sputtering roar. A motorcycle came around the bend behind me driven by a woman in a long gray dress. She pulled up alongside me and stopped.

"In trouble?"

I could, at first, only gape. It wasn't a woman at all, but a monk. There was something comical about the contrast between his gray habit, bare feet in sandals, and white crash helmet.

At last, I said, "You could call it that. My car's got a flat."

He grinned. He was about my age, with an amiable bony face and a big nose on which sat round, steel-rimmed glasses.

"You're an American, aren't you?" he said. "I thought Americans could fix anything."

I started to bristle, but looking at him I found myself smiling instead, in return.

"It shows how wrong you can be," I said. "I thought the English made things that didn't have to be fixed."

"Touché!" he said. "Now the question is, what shall we do to help you, lad? You're a good size but you'll fit on my pillion. Or I could send back help from some garage, but that might not be so certain. Would you trust yourself on my bike?"

"If it'll hold you, I guess it'll hold me. But I don't want to take you out of your way."

"I'm going to Altoncester."

"Maybe you could drop me in Bartonbury. I know there's a service station there."

"Jump on, then."

I tucked my trousers into my socks and got on behind. I hadn't been on a motorbike since my Coast Guard days, and this man drove like he was carrying the good news from Ghent to Aix. I decided, however, that if I wasn't safe with a monk I wasn't going to be safe with anybody, and his Employer was evidently looking after his interests because we got to Bartonbury all in one piece.

It was strange, being back. I stood for a minute in front of the gas station looking towards the long main street of the village. The Cotswold stone houses with their stone-tiled roofs, many green with moss, were warm and inviting in the sunshine; I knew how forbidding they could be when it clouded over. The church tower rose above them, a little askew like a rakish dunce-cap. It, and the stone-pillared market hall, were familiar to me, as familiar as my own village in Connecticut, although I hadn't seen them for over a year. I had left something precious here that made every part of the place rememberable.

"I'll wait for you," my companion said. "If they can't help you, I'll take you on to Altoncester."

I thanked him and went into the garage. I explained what I wanted to the man in charge, who said, in a comfortable Gloucestershire accent, that his young chap was out on a job but would be back after a bit if I cared to wait. I said I would, and returned to the motorcycle.

"I've got a few minutes to wait," I said. "There's somebody I have to see here, but I'd rather get the car settled, first. I'll drive back to it with the repairman."

"Good. You'll be all right, then?"

"Yes. I'll go into the pub. Look, I'm grateful for the lift. I'd like to buy you a drink, but I don't know whether—"

"Oh, yes, we do," he interrupted. "What's the time? Ten-fifteen? Oh, well, it won't matter if I'm a little late."

There was a pub across the street called the Three Horseshoes. He parked his motorbike and we went in. He was my height and we both had to stoop going through the door, which had been made for smaller people. Still hunched, like miners in some ancient seam, we made our way under low beams to a corner of the bar. I bought two pints and we found chairs beside a fireplace in which the only trace of fire was a heap of cigarette butts.

I said, "I can't help being curious about you. I didn't even know there were any monks in England."

"Oh, there are still a goodish number of us." He pulled out a pack of thin, undersized cigarettes and offered me

11

one. "I belong to a teaching order, the Community of the Holy Innocents. We're fairly new, quite small. We have a house not far from Cheltenham, a funny old place. You must come and visit us some day."

"I'd like to. I don't know how long I'll be around."

"Having a holiday?"

"Not exactly. I've come over to try to get somebody to marry me."

He raised his eyebrows. "Couldn't find anyone at home to take a chance?"

"It's not as bad as that. The fact is, she's a girl I met last time I was over here. She lives in Bartonbury."

He nodded, but said nothing.

"You see, my partner and I deal in old books, antiques, and works of art. He's come over several times on buying trips. A year ago I came with him, and we spent some time in this neighborhood. When I met Jill, it was like—well, how can I explain it? I knew this girl was for me. I'd been perfectly happy up to then without being tied down, you know? Or, well," I added, in confusion, "maybe you don't."

His lips twitched. "We're very much like any other men," he said.

"Sorry. I'm hazy about monks. Anyway, before we left I asked her to marry me. She wouldn't."

"She didn't love you?"

"On the contrary, she did. But she couldn't bring herself to leave here. This village, this country, they hold her. Their pull is too strong to escape from. Besides, she has an old aunt who's more or less dependent on her. And she has her own work, part-time teaching with backward kids in Altoncester. So, even though she told me she loved me she just couldn't pull out. I understand. I understood then. But I've had a year to think about it, a year of writing to her every week and getting letters back that tell me she hasn't changed her mind about me—or about the rest of it, either. This year, I made Dave let me make a buying trip. I'm going to have one more try. It it doesn't work—"

12

"You'll go home and try to put her out of your head."

"That's it," I said, glumly. I'd thought it often enough. By now, the decision had become settled in my mind. I was used to it, I lived with it, as you learn to do with an ulcer, for instance.

"It's a hard decision. For both of you," he said. "Do you mind my saying something?"

"Go ahead."

"Sometimes it's better not to bind yourself to a decision before you've explored all the possible avenues—"

I snorted. "There aren't any other possibilities. It's simple. Either she comes with me or she doesn't. What are you thinking of? That I commute between here and Connecticut? I don't make that much money out of the business."

"I can't begin to suggest anything. I don't know anything about either of you. But I do know that when only two alternatives seem to be possible it's usually because we're closing our eyes to a third for some reason. Take me. I was torn between pessimism over the fate of the world and a desire to do something to help set things right. I felt I wanted to teach children how to face the world, but I couldn't bear to face the world myself. My alternatives were, well, to be frank, either to accept some sort of terrible little teaching job in a school where I'd never be able to live on what they paid and where I'd be a sort of inferior servant, or flight from the whole mess—maybe in death. I don't know, perhaps it wouldn't have come to that, but I was pretty desperate. I had forgotten the third possibility: God."

"Becoming a monk solved everything?"

"Oh, no. It opened up a whole new range of problems. But the original dilemma was solved when I saw that I could live both in and out of the world. That's a simplification, of course. But what I mean is that there was another avenue for me, only I didn't see it until I had my eyes properly open."

"You're telling me to pray, I suppose," I said. "It's not

13

my dish. A long time ago, missionaries read a couple of pages of the New Testament to a great Cherokee Indian chief named Yanugunski. He said, 'It seems to be a pretty good book. It is strange that since the white people have had it so long they are no better than they are.' "

He looked at me with a new concentration, and I knew he was suddenly seeing the shape of my eyes and my color. "Are you a Red Indian?" he asked.

"My father was a full-blooded Cherokee. My mother was half and half."

"Gosh! Excuse my curiosity. We used to play Red Indians when I was a kid—well, you know. Did you live on a reservation?"

"There isn't any reservation for the Cherokees. We were just pushed off our lands and given nothing in return. I was born in Oklahoma, if that means anything to you."

He said, doubtfully, "It's in the Far West, I suppose."

"Not exactly." I couldn't help grinning. "But it's about as dusty as a desert. We were luckier than most. My father was a lawyer, and during the war he got to know someone in the Judge Advocate General's office, a New Englander, who must have persuaded him to move because after the war, when I was nine, we went east to Hartford, in Connecticut. That's where I grew up. We had my grandfather with us, a great old man. I loved him. He taught me all about Indian history, and never let me forget what I was. Not that I needed much reminding."

"What do you mean?"

I said, bitterly, "Some of the kids in my neighborhood didn't like dark skins. 'Nig' was what they used to call me. There's a kind of justice in that, I guess, because when the Cherokees lived in Georgia they were slave-owners."

"Didn't you ever feel you wanted to go back to—er—Oklahoma?"

"If we'd stayed there, we'd have been called dirty Indians. No, I liked it in Connecticut all right. It was a lot greener than Stillwater. And of course when I was older, things changed."

14

He drew a long breath. "How interesting. I never thought I'd actually meet a Red Indian."

"Well, don't let it throw you. I never thought I'd meet a monk."

"I'm sorry about my outburst. It was bad manners. I have no business telling you what to do." He sounded genuinely contrite.

I said, quickly, "Not at all. I appreciate the sense of what you said, even though it won't work in my case."

"I didn't mean that my solution would apply to you. I only meant that we tend to blind ourselves, involuntarily perhaps, to the most obvious way out of a difficulty simply because something in us isn't ready to accept it. But there, I've talked enough. Brother Simon is always on at me about my nattering."

He finished off his beer and rose, holding out a hand. "It's been very pleasant meeting you, Mr.—I don't even know your name."

"Eddison. Bob Eddison."

"Oh." He looked disappointed, and I guessed why.

So I said, "My Cherokee name is Ahuludegi. It means Big Hawk." Actually, it means He Throws Away the Drum, but I knew Big Hawk was more the kind of thing he'd expect.

And indeed, he looked much happier. "Splendid," he said. "And mine's Anselm. I hope you'll visit us before you go."

"The Community of the—?"

"Holy Innocents. I'm not sure that doesn't have vaguely satirical overtones. It's two miles from Cheltenham. Anyone can tell you where it is."

We went crouching out under the beams like a pair of Richard the Thirds, and he glanced at his wristwatch.

"Help! I'm going to have to hurry. Still, I suppose the viewing or sighting or whatever they call it will go on for quite a while."

"Viewing?" I pricked up my ears like a good little dealer. "You're going to an auction?"

15

"The auction's tomorrow. There's a dear old soul who's always looking after us. She thinks of us as her special charges. And she's offered to put up the money for some bookcases for the community. There's one coming up for sale at the auction and I'm going to look at it today and see if it's big enough."

"So it's just a furniture auction?"

"Oh, no, there are all sorts of things. Books, kitchen utensils, garden tools, paintings—"

"Where is this?"

"At the Corn Hall in Altoncester."

"Tomorrow, eh? Maybe I ought to take a look. Good things sometimes turn up at these country auctions."

"Then I may see you there if we decide to bid for the bookcases."

"Maybe. And don't worry. Viewings go on all day, so you'll have plenty of time."

He got on his motorcycle and kicked the starter. "Good luck," he said, over the roar. "Keep your eyes open for the third possibility."

The repairman had returned to the garage and I drove out to my car with him. I was back in Bartonbury twenty minutes later. I parked on Silver Street in front of the well-remembered house. Its thatch gleamed like patinated old pewter. Its silvery beams and worn plaster were set off by a hedge of box, and by beds of flowers and a couple of untidy rosebushes. It looked as unreal as a greeting card from some Never Never Land of Merrie Englande, but I knew that inside it was chilly, damp and darkish, that the furniture was too big for the small rooms, and that Jill's aunt, Miss Trout, gave her horse tea in the kitchen.

I had cabled Jill to say I was coming, but I hadn't been sure what day. I knew I should have phoned but some childish notion of surprising her had kept me from doing so. And also, I was nervous. I was more nervous than I'd thought possible. My throat felt raw and the pulse in it thumped solemnly. I felt as if I were going in for a crucial medical examination: Now, Mr. Eddison, how long have you had this pain in the heart?

I went through the gate at last and knocked at the door. Miss Trout opened to me. She was a rawboned woman, not as old as she looked, in her late fifties but already very gray and lined. Over her skirt and sweater she wore a frilly apron, and over that a green cardigan eaten by moth. Instead of shoes, she wore a pair of red plastic boots. Her pale blue eyes had a kindly but unfocused look and I knew from experience that she lived in a world vaguer than other people's.

So I wasn't surprised when she exclaimed, "Heavens! You'll be wanting the cakes and I haven't finished icing them yet."

"No, Miss Trout," I said. "I'm Bob Eddison."

"There's no Mr. Eddison on my list," she said. "But how absurd of me! Lady Cowleigh said she'd send someone for the cakes—for the Women's Institute show, you know—but of course she meant one of the ladies. Won't you come in?"

She held the door wide and I went in, automatically ducking because of beams. She led the way along the passage through a cosy baking smell. The back of the house was taken up by a large, comfortable room which was used as much for a sitting-room as for a kitchen, and, as I had expected, the horse, Solomon, was standing at the back door, his head in the room although the rest of him was too big to get through the opening. I said hello to him.

Miss Trout said, "I expect you'll have come about the Scouts."

"I've come to see Jill," I said, patiently.

"Jill? My niece? But she has nothing to do with the Scouts."

"It's not about the Scouts, Miss Trout. I'm Bob Eddison. From the United States. Don't you remember me? I'm the one who wants to marry her."

She stroked her forhead. "I really must be losing my

17

wits," she said. "Of course I remember you. It's having to get the baking done at the last minute that's driven everything else out of my head. I had thought I'd have another day or two at least."

She held out her hand to me then, and I took it. "How are you, Mr. Eddison? And how's your nice friend, Mr. Canfield?"

"Cannon. He's fine. Where's Jill?"

"Now, my dear, let me think a moment. It's so unexpected, your turning up like this. Jill told me something—"

"She's not here?" I said, with a sinking at the gut.

"Oh, no. Where did I put—? Ah, yes." From the dresser she fetched a piece of paper and held it out to me. I recognized my cable.

Coming England June 15, I had said. *Must Spend Half Business But Other Half You Love Bob.*

Beneath this, Jill had written, "Bob darling, I waited for you to phone. Didn't know where to reach you. I had to go on a five-day course in Sussex for teachers who work with problem children. I'll phone Aunt Grace every evening in case you've come. I'll be back on the 23rd. Can't wait to see you. All my love."

So there I was. Big surprise, but in reverse. The truth was, I had been afraid to phone, afraid she'd say no even before I could see her. Today was the twenty-first. I had spent five whole days visiting dealers in London and dawdling around the sale-rooms when I could have been here, making my pitch. No wonder the Indians had lost North America.

Miss Trout had been watching me sympathetically, and she said, "I'm so sorry, my dear. You've missed her. What would you like to do?"

What I would have liked to do was give myself a swift kick in the ass. However, I merely answered, "I'll hang around. I'll go to a hotel somewhere and register and then let you know where I am so you can tell Jill." I crossed my fingers, hoping she'd remember who I was when I phoned, and that she'd get the number right.

18

Then I recalled what Brother Anselm had told me about the auction. It would at least give me something to do that would come under the heading of business rather than time-wasting.

"I'll go to Altoncester," I said. "If I could just use your phone—"

"Certainly."

I got the Altoncester book and looked up hotels. There was a Trust House there, the White Swan. I rang them and was able to book a room. Then, on the back of the cablegram, I wrote out the hotel's number.

"There," I said. "That's where I'll be. When Jill phones tonight, you just read this out to her. You won't forget?"

"Heavens, no. I'll put it right here on the shelf where I'll be sure to see it. And," she added, gaily, "if I do forget, Solomon will remind me."

I nodded. I had done all I could.

Altoncester was a kind of object lesson in what the English were capable of doing to their country. I drove past bleak-looking council houses in long rows, a miniature Levittown of fake Cotswold stone punctuated by factories, a ball-bearing plant, a valve manufacturer, a body shop; then grimy ranks of Victorian cottages, their doors painted blue or yellow, lace curtains in the windows, and each with its hopeful name, something like Bonny Brae or Fairdene. Then came the heart of the town with its narrow, winding streets and its old houses, some half-timbered, many fine Jacobean stone, but all now become Ann's Pantry, Woolworth's, Boots', Genuine Sales, Olde Worlde Antiques, Photographic Chemists, Fish & Chips, and so on. Traffic jammed the quaint old streets, and I oozed along with the flow of drivers wistfully searching for the Grail of an empty parking space, while about us the incense of our engine exhausts rose on the summer air.

My hotel, fortunately, had once been a coaching inn and had a courtyard in which I could leave my car. I signed in, left my bag, and went to find the Corn Hall.

It wasn't hard to find. It fronted the market square, itself square, solid and plain, a testimony to the prosperous farmers who had erected it under the long Georgian rule. It held itself haughtily above their descendants, who had filled the streets and the marketplace with shoddy goods and farting cars.

The main room inside was an immense, high-ceilinged auditorium with a stage, used generally, I suppose, for town meetings. Today, however, it was as packed with goods as any flea market, and every inch that wasn't things was people looking at things. I searched around for Brother Anselm but didn't see him, so I began threading my way through the crowd.

I could discount most of the stuff. I wasn't interested in bound sets of *The Gentleman's Magazine* with the volume for 1911 missing, or in slightly chipped Worcester services for twenty people, or in mahogany sideboards, or cast iron firebacks, or imitation Tiffany glass, or even real Tiffany glass. I passed up tables full of kitchenware mixed with old microscopes, African carvings made in Hong Kong, engraved fish knives in plush-lined cases, and Victorian decanters with the wrong stoppers. There were some good lots, although they weren't my sort of thing: a couple of pieces of Waterford crystal, some Staffordshire, some nice jewelry. Along the walls behind the fringed and silk-shaded floor lamps and the oak dressers and the stacks of chairs were hung pictures. Most of them were crude enough junk, or even reproductions; some of the big ones would be bought for the gold leaf in the frames. However, there were some landscapes which weren't too bad, and a number of miniatures, including a few definitely saleable ones. I looked carefully at these. There was a dresser to one side of them with a big hinged mirror standing on it, and this made it difficult to get close to the miniatures. I squeezed up alongside it, and then I saw that hanging behind the mirror and almost completely concealed by it was a small painting.

It was hard to get at but I managed to unhook it from the wall. When I had it in the light, I stared at it and all I wanted to say was, "What's a nice kid like you doing in a place like this?"

It was no more than ten by twelve but it had a wonderful spaciousness. That quality of open air within small boundaries said *Dutch* almost before you saw the careful handling of details and the melting blues and soft greens. On a hillock in the foreground were a couple of big,

21

gnarled trees, their foliage touched by sunlight over dark shadow. Beyond were level meadows through which wound a stream reflecting the clouds and the pale watery sky. At the edge of the meadows you could make out the roofs of a town and the sails of a windmill. And under the trees, a man in a red coat was aiming a crossbow at a crow which had just flown from a branch. That one rich spot of red focused the whole picture and gave it its depth.

It had been done by a real painter, all right. There was no signature but it even looked vaguely familiar, as if, given a hint, I might guess his name. I said to myself, seventeenth-century Dutch. Then I looked some more and felt uneasy. Just because it was good I mistrusted it. I am far from being an expert on pictures, although we sell quite a few, and I couldn't believe that a seventeenth-century Dutch painting would turn up in this rat's nest. Such bargains don't exist.

I turned it over. Pasted on the back of the panel, and partly obscured by dirt, was a small piece of paper. The writing on it was faded and brown, but with my pocket magnifier I was able to read it.

Copied, it said, *from the painting by Jan van der Heyden, Gal. Sab. Turin. H. T. Maxwell, 1879.*

I told you so, I said. Nevertheless, copy or no copy, it was an attractive, well-painted picture. What's more, I had a customer for it, a man who would buy it as a nineteenth-century oddity. His name was McLeod, a Connecticut businessman, rich, nearing retirement, who was interested in works of art and was one of our regulars. He'd pay a couple of hundred for it. And if he didn't want it, I'd keep it myself provided I could get it cheaply enough.

I had bought a catalogue for five pence, half a dozen mimeographed sheets stapled together. I looked up Lot 387. "Dutch school. Landscape in oils on panel." No mention of H. T. Maxwell, of course, and none needed. Anybody in the trade would find out as quickly as I had.

And anybody in the trade would know, as I did, that

with the identifying bit of paper scraped off the back, the picture would move up in the world. That it wasn't already off I could probably put down to the confusion or ineptitude of country auctioneers.

I hung it up again, carefully, behind the mirror. There was no point in calling attention to it. That was part of the game, too.

I noted it and the miniatures and one or two other little things in my catalogue. Then I pushed my way out. I stood on the steps of the Corn Hall for a few minutes, glad to be out of the fug of human bodies, breathing in the alternate richness of burned gasoline just tinged with sulphur dioxide that must have come from one of the factories on the edge of town. The rest of the day stretched before me, pure nothing, until Jill should phone.

I remembered that there was an antique dealer in Altoncester who was a friend of Dave's. I had met him a year ago, a man named Reggie West, an agreeable type, very neat, dapper, and knowledgeable. After a bite of lunch, I strolled over to his shop, introduced myself, and passed a pleasant enough hour. I bought a couple of good silver boxes and a fine Limoges candlestick at reasonable prices, so the day couldn't be considered a total loss.

Jill, I knew, phoned her aunt about six. Six, accordingly, found me waiting in my hotel room. By seven, tired of staring at the obstinately mute telephone, I called Miss Trout.

"Oh, yes, Mr. Eddison," she said. "Jill rang about an hour ago."

"And you gave her my number?"

"The one on the telegram? Yes, indeed."

"Well, what did she say?"

"She asked how I was feeling, and I told her about the Women's Institute sale—"

"I don't mean that. Did she say she'd phone me?"

"No, I don't think so. I told her you wanted to marry her. That was right, wasn't it?"

"Oh, sure, that's fine. How did she take it?"

"She said, 'Oh, dear.' "

"Oh dear? She said that?" Suddenly, I wasn't amused. "Is that all she said?"

"It wasn't a very long conversation. Hasn't she phoned you yet?"

"No."

"I suppose she must be tied up. She's been kept terribly busy with her course."

"Yes. I see."

I thought I did see. I hung up. brooding. This was a brush-off, wasn't it? "Oh, dear." That spelled, How am I going to tell him that I still don't want to marry him? Better not to phone. Better to let the whole thing die quietly, like a poisoned mouse.

But her note, I reminded myself, hadn't given that impression. Why phone every evening in case I'd come? Why say, "Can't wait to see you?"

Maybe, I thought, she's dead. Maybe as she left the phone booth a truck ran her down and at this moment she's lying in a hospital morgue, bleeding and silent.

Or maybe, on the other hand, she couldn't wait to see me because she had something unpleasant to tell me and wanted to get it over with. Another guy, somebody at the course, some sharp young teacher with a luxuriant beard setting off his bloodless skin. Indians have almost no hair on their faces. And I am nearly as dark as my father, and he was what my grandfather Astugataga used to call *tsolaga yonli*, old tobacco.

She might be seeing him now, that hairy pale man, asking him what she ought to do, whether to phone me and finish it or wait and let me down more easily when she returned.

All right, I said, resolutely. We'll see. I'll give her another half hour and if she doesn't phone, we're finished.

At ten-thirty, having read the new Simenon I'd bought that afternoon, and worked my way through the Book of Kings in the Gideon Bible next to the bed, I went down to the hotel bar and had a couple of double whiskies. Then I

24

went back upstairs with a copy of last year's *Punch* and eventually fell into a restless, angry sleep.

I woke late, with the taste of stale magazine jokes in my mouth. I felt anti-English. Lying in bed I enumerated grievances: the overdone menu of the hotel's dinner, full of French euphemisms for breaded veal cutlets or shrimps and rice, the overdone tournedos I had eaten, the tiny weak whiskies I had drunk, the lumpy bed, the absence of a bed lamp, the incomprehensibility of *Punch* and of the English in general and Jill in particular. I wanted to go back to good old Connecticut, with its poison ivy, its tent caterpillars, its landscape of billboards and gas stations and hamburger joints, its maddening commuter trains and its frightened commuters.

No, I thought, the fact is I don't much care for anybody today. Not my day. I should have been born two hundred years ago, when I could have followed the trail or made pemmican or whatever we noble redmen did when we weren't sleeping off our liquor.

I made myself get up. The sale began at ten and it was already nearly nine. Not that it mattered that much: there were more than five hundred lots, and since professional auctioneers average about a hundred lots an hour it would be a full day's entertainment. As I dressed I debated phoning Miss Trout again, but to what purpose? No, I'd wait and give Jill some more time. Maybe by this evening she'd ring up, or maybe by the time the auction was over there'd be a message for me at the desk.

I went over to the Corn Hall after breakfast. The big room seemed emptier than it had been at the viewing. Chairs had been squeezed in, in various places, and it was the fact that a lot of people were sitting down that made it seem less crowded. The auctioneer had already begun rattling through the first lots. I spotted Reggie perched on a dower chest tagged Lot 181 and went over to join him.

"You'll have to be on your toes if you want anything," he said. "There's a London chap here, and that lot generally have their pockets stuffed with lolly."

25

"Where is he?"

He pointed to a thin, blond man wearing heavily black-rimmed glasses.

"He owns a gallery in Davies Street called the Scampi. He has a relation in Altoncester and comes up now and again on buying trips."

"I know him by sight," I said. "I think Dave and I bought something from him last time. What about the locals?"

"Plenty of them here, too. They always come along to these things. It's the jewelry and silver they're after. I don't doubt there'll be a ring," he added, bitterly. "Makes it bloody hard for chaps like me. I don't go in for that sort of thing myself."

He was referring to the system by which several dealers agree to let one of their number bid for all, thus cutting down the competition and squeezing out opposition. Then they auction the prize among themselves, the top bidder paying off the rest. Auction houses are always claiming that the rings have been stamped out, but they might as well claim to have stamped out houseflies over garbage cans.

The auctioneer worked his way around to some of the furniture. When he came to "a bookcase, glass-fronted, three shelves, in good order, a bit of a crack in one of the panes but nothing a handyman can't mend," I looked for Brother Anselm among the bidders. He wasn't there, and I supposed it hadn't been what he wanted.

The furniture moved fast and we got to some fairly nice silver. Reggie tried for a Georgian dredger and I could see that there must indeed be a ring because after the usual jokers dropped out—the people who tried for it at two or three pounds—the bidding, instead of being from a half dozen dealers, was confined to Reggie and one other person, a fat man who needed a shave. The price went up and up, and at £110 Reggie dropped out.

"It's diabolical!" he growled. "If the bidding were properly spread, I should have had it for seventy-five."

The problem about the competition of the sale-room is that you must always be figuring your profit. As the price rises, you have to keep computing. Otherwise, you may find yourself landed with something that can sit around in your inventory for five years. I looked over at the fat man and wondered whether his crowd wanted pictures.

Reggie was forced out of the next thing he wanted, and then came back strongly for a pair of early George Two trencher salts, which he got for a hundred and five pounds.

"Too high, but it's a matter of principle," he muttered. "And I have an American who may buy them."

There was more silver to come later. The auctioneer moved on to the miniatures and I had a chance to see how workmanlike the London man from the Scampi Gallery could be. There were eight miniatures. Six were late nine-teenth-century, without much merit, but there was a good seventeenth-century one on copper, and a fine delicate one by a Spanish artist dated 1807. Mr. Scampi let the poor ones go, and then took the Spanish one away from the fat man, nonchalantly pushing the price up with almost imper-ceptible nods and great speed. I came in on the bidding for the seventeenth-century portrait just to show Scampi that I meant business. The ring man, sweating, had shaken his head at forty pounds and I took over. I got it for sixty. Scampi glanced over one shoulder at me with a faint smile, and I saw the fat man and several others looking at me, too. Now they knew I was here, a stranger, with some serious money.

We got through three hundred lots and stopped briefly for refreshment. A bar had been set up in an adjoining room, and Reggie and I had a sandwich and some beer. They started again with a second auctioneer, and by about two-thirty we had come to Lot 387.

They had a bit of trouble finding it at first, behind the mirror. That meant either that no one else had seen it, or whoever had seen it had thoughtfully returned it to obscurity, as I had. Seeing it again, as the auctioneer's assistant held it up. I liked it even more. Its soft colors

27

glowed in the harsh lighting of the hall. Even its frame was good, an early carved and gilded one.

Reggie stirred beside me, and said, "Where did that come from? I never noticed it."

I said nothing. It would have been improper for me to tell him I wanted it. He'd find out soon enough, and then he could decide for himself whether to bid against me or not. The chances were that since he hadn't examined it, he wouldn't stay anyway.

"A very attractive little work," the auctioneer was saying, "and who'll open the bidding at twenty pounds?"

There was silence, and then one of the jokers said, "Ten shillings."

"Fifty new pence," the auctioneer said, reprovingly. "Come, gentlemen, let's be serious."

A few others brought it up to three pounds, and then the ring man came in. He said, "Eight," thus announcing that he was going to make it five pound bids and that anybody who wasn't serious had better pick up his hat.

A loud voice across the room said, "Ten."

The auctioneer glanced that way, repeating, "Ten pounds."

The bidder had raised his hand for attention, and I could mark him. I could see a tweed jacket, a silk scarf under the collar of a Tattersall shirt, a healthy-looking, high-colored face, graying blond hair. It was hard to say why, but even in that glimpse I got a sense of assurance that verged on arrogance.

The fat man said fifteen and the other seventeen. That was interesting. He was refusing to be drawn into the five-pound jumps. The auctioneer accepted it. The bid was Fatso's and I saw him pause. He whispered to someone next to him and I suspected he hadn't seen the painting before. With what looked like reluctance, he stayed in.

"Twenty-four," said the tweedy man, still moving by twos.

28

Fatso shook his head.

At this point, the London man joined. He lifted a finger, and said, "Twenty-five."

I felt it was now time for me to take a hand. I knew Scampi had seen the picture or he never would have bothered. I intended to show him that I was prepared to take it. I was pretty sure I could get $150 from McLeod for it, that is, about £60, maybe somewhat more. I could certainly get more if I scraped the label off the back, but both Dave and I have strong feelings about honesty; we like to stand behind our descriptions of what we sell.

I said, "Thirty."

"Thirty pounds against the wall," said the auctioneer. He looked at Scampi. "Will you say thirty-five, sir?"

Scampi didn't move for a second or two. His pause told me he was making the same calculations I was. It might be a lot of money for what was, after all, a copy even if a good one. Then he nodded. He was probably going to take the label off the back.

I at once gave my own signal.

Scampi shot me a look and shrugged. Pictures were not what his gallery usually handled.

"Are we all through at forty pounds?" said the auctioneer.

The tweedy man put his hand up. "Forty-five," he said.

He took me by surprise. I had forgotten all about him. I looked over that way. I was sure he wasn't a dealer. Maybe he was just used to having his own way.

I said, "Fifty."

"Fifty-five."

This was annoying. I was going over my limit. And I saw Scampi's head turn and realized that he was asking himself whether he had missed something, whether it might be a better buy than he had thought. If he came back in and I had to deal with both of them, I'd have to let it go.

I nodded at the auctioneer.

There was a pause.

"It's with you, sir," the auctioneer said to the tweedy man.

I saw him crane his neck to stare at me over the crowd. Then he said, "Sixty-five."

I clenched my teeth and nodded again immediately, to push him.

"The bid is seventy pounds. Any more, sir?"

My opponent opened his mouth and shut it again.

"Going once at seventy pounds."

For a moment, I thought the tweedy man was going to change his mind. But he folded his arms sullenly.

"Twice. No more? Yours, sir," the auctioneer said, pointing his hammer at me.

"Good show," said Reggie

I had a little trouble unclenching my teeth. I had been drawn into something I rarely did—overbidding out of pure anger and rivalry. I had paid $170 for a gamble, about fifty bucks more than I had intended.

"Now I know how you felt," I said to Reggie. "Damn all matters of principle."

I was waiting at the desk to pay for my lots when the tweedy man appeared beside me. He was as tall as I, which was why I had been able to see him over the crowd, but heavier, mostly in the middle. I don't mean fat; he was just solid and substantial, as a man and a citizen.

He said, "Sorry to trouble you. May I have a word with you?"

"Sure," I said. "Let me collect my stuff."

I got the painting and the miniature, gave them a check drawn on the external account we keep in England for such purposes, and went to join him in the corner to which he had withdrawn.

"My name's Villiers," he said, not offering to shake hands. "I gather you're an American dealer, is that so?"

"That's right."

"Now, Mr.—ah—"

"Eddison."

"Mr. Eddison. About that little painting you've bought. I wonder if I could possibly persuade you to part with it. It has a strong sentimental attachment for me."

I raised my eyebrows. "I'm afraid I'm not in business for sentimental reasons."

"I understand. But you see, it belonged to a friend of mine who is dead. A very dear friend. It would be all I'd have to remember him by."

He looked sincere, and maybe it was true. But sentiment or no sentiment, I didn't like the fact that he had pushed

31

me above the limit I'd set myself.

Then he added, with an engaging smile, "If we had met beforehand, you see, I'd have asked you not to bid against me."

I said, with restraint, "Some people might think that was unethical."

He gave a laugh. When he laughed, his shoulders jerked up and down as if he were emphasizing just how hearty his hilarity was.

"Oh, please, let's not mention ethics," he said. "I come up against a lot of you fellows. Your ethics only apply to each other, not to the poor customer. Isn't that so?"

He had a loud voice and I don't like loud voices. I gave him a small piece of sour smile.

"As it happens, I don't think I want to sell it," I said.

"Naturally, I'd be willing to pay you a little something over your price." He managed to make it sound like Louis XIV giving somebody permission to kiss his hand.

I retorted, "I've already paid a hell of a lot over my price."

That brought him up short. He said, stiffly, "I see. How much do you expect to get for it?"

All right, whiteface, I said, now I'm going to teach you a lesson. *Hilagu?* How much?

"Five hundred dollars," I said it with that impassivity Dave likes to think of as particularly Indian, and which I acquired when I was being knuckled by the older kids in school.

Villiers stared at me. "Five hundred—? That's two hundred pounds. Preposterous!"

"Do you think so?" I said. "In that case, I'm sorry. No sale."

"But look here. It's only a copy. That's a ridiculous sum to pay for a nineteenth-century copy. It's highway robbery."

I was beginning to take a real dislike to him by now. I don't like being heckled by buyers or told how to run my affairs. I didn't think he was serious about buying the picture unless he could get it for a trifle over what I'd paid for it. And I didn't think I believed that story about the dead friend.

I said, "Nobody's asking you to pay it. If you'll excuse me—"

I started to move away. He stepped in front of me.

He said, in a voice which he was obviously struggling to keep mild and pacific, "Just a moment. I have a suggestion to make."

I expected him to offer to split the difference. I waited.

He said, "Let me ask you something. You haven't any special feeling for that particular painting, have you? I mean to say, since you're a dealer all you're interested in is getting your money. Right?"

"Wrong. I do have a special feeling for this painting. But go on."

"Well, now, you know two hundred pounds is a frightfully high price. On the other hand, as I have told you, I have a strong reason for wanting it. I have a rather good collection of pictures. Suppose I were to offer you an exchange—a swap?"

Of all the things I had expected, this was the last. And it was also the one guaranteed to be irresistible. I have always been a swapper. I treasure the memory of glorious swaps the way some people remember the fight a five-pound trout put up. When I was only twelve I traded a Scout knife for a shiny little coin another kid had which turned out to be a ten-dollar gold piece from his father's collection. My mother made me give it back, but the thrill of the game had caught me and it never let me go.

Just the same, I am a cautious man. There was something a trifle fishy here. I said, "It's an interesting idea. I never say no to a swap. But if I understand you, you're willing to trade me a picture I can make two hundred pounds from, yet you won't pay the price for this one."

He cleared his throat. He said, "You must realize, I can't guarantee that you'll find a picture you want in my collection which will bring you two hundred pounds. No. But

33

prices are considerably higher in your country for—ah—paintings that might qualify as antiques rather than as outstanding works of art."

He was saying that there are more suckers in America than in England. Well, maybe he was right. But I also got something else. I felt sure he didn't have two hundred pounds in cash.

I found the situation intriguing. He looked like a country squire, a man reasonably well off. And indeed, he had bid over a hundred and fifty dollars for this painting, knowing what it was. Sentiment? He had—or said he had—a good collection of paintings. That meant his eye might be a lot better than mine. Did he see something I was missing? He wouldn't meet my price. Well, admittedly it was stiff. I know that rich people are more sensitive than others about spending money. But he was willing to trade something that had to be fairly good. What, I asked myself, did he have in mind?

I said, "It won't hurt for me to look at what you've got, I suppose. Where do you live?"

"Not very far, at least by your American standards. About fifteen miles away. All right?"

"Okay."

"You do have a car? That's all right, then. You can follow me."

"You want to go now?"

"If you've no objection."

His car was parked in a lot near the hotel. As I might have guessed, it was a Jag. An elderly one, however, and showing traces of a hard life. I got my car and started after him.

We drove north, along one of the ruled Roman roads that led out of Altoncester like the spokes of a wheel. We turned off on a narrow lane sunk between hedgerows, dropped down to cross a stone bridge over a wide, shallow river, and began to climb. I caught glimpses over the hedges or walls of a panorama of fields, sewn together like patchwork by other walls and hedges, dropping away

34

further and further below me as I drove, crowned here and there by clumps of trees. We passed through a hamlet called Upper Brook, no more than a squat church and four houses. A few miles further, a black-lettered road sign said *Chaworth*.

We drove along the main street of one of the most attractive villages I'd ever seen, a real cliché out of a Beautiful Britain calendar. Every house was made of ancient stone and tiled with stone, some with bits and pieces of medieval carvings embedded in their walls, many with the fine pillared doorways of the eighteenth century added to older structures. Through openings or lanes between the houses I caught glimpses of gardens full of summer color. The street widened to embrace a market hall with a Tudor clock and a rambling hotel with its name in gilded letters fastened across the front: King's Head. To the right, the square Norman tower of the church rose above sway-backed roofs. Then we were on the other side and were passing rows of houses in a development, clean but dull, two-storied, each with its tiny swatch of lawn in front, its bicycle and baby carriage, and two empty milk bottles on the door step.

Beyond this drab girdle lay open country. We turned into a wooded road and came to a large house standing among beeches and chestnuts. Villiers stopped in the drive and I pulled up behind him.

"That was a pretty village," I said, as we got out.

"Ah, yes. But terribly old-fashioned, I'm afraid. Come inside."

I followed him into the hall. A woman came out of a side room as he shut the door, and said, "Oh, it's you."

They exchanged glances in which I read nothing but dislike.

Then, turning to me with his face arranged in a smile, he said, "This is my wife. Mr. Eddison, my dear."

She was rather plump, with a lovely complexion and sullen, dark eyes. A few gray hairs, a few lines around mouth and eyes told me she wasn't as young as she

35

dressed, but the total effect was attractive.

"Mr. Eddison is an American," Villiers went on. "He's come to look at my collection."

She gave me her hand, and with it a long, slow, appraising look as if she was trying to bring me into focus. Her hand clung to mine and I suddenly had the panicky feeling that she was going to twine around me like a vine.

"I'm sure you'd like some tea," she said. "I'll call you when it's ready."

She said it the way a woman who has invited you in for a drink says, "I'll slip into something comfortable."

She let go of me then, and I went with Villiers into a large room that looked out on a flagged terrace. Its walls were paneled, and there was only one painting in the room, a large dark portrait of a man in an embroidered waistcoat and a periwig, hanging over the fireplace.

"A Kneller," Villiers remarked. "I picked it up a few years ago, one winter, at an auction in the Corn Hall. An auction like today's, except that the weather was very bad and I had no competition."

"Lucky you," I said. "Is that your collection?"

He chuckled. "Only part of it. You see, Mr. Eddison, I have a feeling that art is important. I don't consider good paintings to be a kind of wallpaper. If you are one of those people who play a Bach fugue on the gramophone as background music to a cocktail party, you won't appreciate my point. I like to bring my full attention to bear on a painting when I look at it, and I like others to do so as well. Since most people aren't prepared for such concentration I'd rather not have them look at all."

I said, "I knew a man once who felt that too much looking at paintings wore their surfaces away."

He decided that that was meant to be funny, and smiled. Then he walked over to one of the sections of paneling and, setting his fingers into a recess alongside one of the carved mouldings, pulled the whole thing away from the wall. It was hinged. A light snapped on and illuminated the space behind, where six or eight small pictures hung.

I let my impassivity slip. "Very interesting. And the rest of the paneling?"

He strode around the room pulling at alternate panels until six had been opened. He had told nothing but the truth. He did indeed have a pretty good collection.

I could see at once that about half the pictures were Dutch. There were some drawings, some watercolors, and some oils. Most were late, and some were clearly no more than good decorative hackwork, but there were a few real mouth-waterers. There were perhaps twenty altogether, and they made up a very respectable if small collection. The rest of the pictures were English, mainly nineteenth-century landscapes. It was all neatly labeled, which was a help because I don't know much about Dutch art. However, even I could recognize some of the names: a water-color of a church interior by Bosboom, a small landscape by Jacob Cats, an oil sketch by van Drielst.

I said, "You must have spent a fortune on some of this stuff."

"Not at all," he replied. "Most of my Dutch things go back a few years. You used to be able to pick them up at reasonable prices. The later Hollanders were looked down on. Try to find a book about Dutch art, even today, in London, and you'll have difficulty. Even if you do find one it will go no further than Vermeer, probably. It's only recently, since other things have disappeared, that the Dutch artists have begun to fetch high prices."

"I see. You really are drawn to these Dutchmen, aren't you?"

"They impose order on nature," he said.

"And that's why you want my painting?"

"Not at all. I told you, it belonged to a dear friend. Well," he added, his color deepening, "yes, perhaps the fact that it is a copy of a Dutch painting adds to its sentimental value. You'll notice that it's copied from a van der Heyden in Turin. I may even have seen that original."

37

He beckoned me to one of the panels on the fireplace wall. "Now here's something you might be interested in. I thought of this as a possible exchange."

It was a rosy-cheeked country girl standing for some reason in shrubbery up to her waist, and looking reproachfully heavenward as if at some passing, diarrheic bird.

"It's by H. E. Hobson," Villiers explained. "Very well known man. It's dated 1860."

"No," I said.

"But in today's market it must be worth a hundred pounds."

"Not to me."

He showed me a few more of that sort, working his way up to some cows standing knee deep in a pool beneath purple mountains' majesty, by an R.A. named Alfred de Breanski.

"No," I said. I still liked my own painting, copy or no copy. But if his swaps didn't interest me his behavior did, for he began to lose his cool and to display a certain impatience, even feverishness about pressing me into some kind of trade.

For one thing, he began offering me better works. He was now up to a large watercolor by Copley Fielding, a picture of real quality, and he passed from that to a Rowlandson wash drawing which I knew by the most conservative estimate ought to bring two hundred and fifty pounds.

And that was too much. I was brought up to be wary. My grandfather Astugataga used to tell me stories about Indian history. In them, the white faces always came offering all sorts of wonderful things in exchange for mere nothings like the right to hunt on Indian land, or maybe just the right to cross it. In the end, the Indians were always left with a handful of sheath knives and two bottles of booze, in exchange for which they found they had given away their lands, their homes, and their hunting grounds. I tend to freeze up when somebody starts urging me to take something for nothing just because he has a defect of personality that makes him altruistic.

Here was Villiers, the friend of the Red Man, having begun by not wanting to pay five hundred dollars for something that might not be worth two hundred, now offering me in effect six hundred and fifty for it.

I said, "Mr. Villiers, that's very tempting. But I'll tell you something. I don't think I want to swap."

He stared at me. "Look here," he said, his voice loud again, "you can't do that. That Rowlandson's genuine. I consider it more than a fair trade for that wretched painting. You'd be a fool to pass it up."

Clearly, he didn't realize what he was saying. And I wasn't going to bring it to his attention. But I thought, *"Curiouser and curiouser."*

"That's right," I said, winningly. "You're absolutely right. What I meant was that I don't want to swap this minute. Let me think about it. Okay?"

"But aren't you leaving Altoncester?" he asked.

"I'll be here for another day or two."

His wife appeared at the door and said that tea was ready. With an annoyed gesture, Villiers motioned me to precede him. We went into a pleasant little sitting room lined with bookshelves, the windows open to a walled garden resounding with bees. Mrs. Villiers sat me in an easy chair and began filling a plate for me with thin bread and butter and biscuits.

"What do you do, Mr. Eddison?" she said.

"I'm a dealer in antiques and works of art," I answered. "That's how I met your husband. We were bidding against each other at the auction today for a little painting."

"Oh, Charles and his paintings," she said, her eyes darting towards him. "Which of you won?"

He stirred his tea sulkily.

"I did, I'm afraid," I said.

I saw her lips twitch as if she were fighting a smile. "Dear me. Don't tell me it was that picture of George's, Charles.

39

He went down expressly to try to get it," she added to me.

I said, "And was this friend of yours a big collector of paintings too, Mr. Villiers?"

"George Puncheon was a big collector of everything." His shoulders performed their saltatory accompaniment to laughter. "He could afford to be. He collected money as well, you see."

"I see. Then he did have a lot of pictures."

"I'll tell you about George," Villiers said, putting down his cup and bringing out a box of long, thin cigars. "He specialized in masterpieces. He had a theory that there were hundreds of lost works, fine paintings which had been brought here during the eighteenth and early nineteenth centuries by young men who made the Grand Tour, and which had been dispersed owing to the changes in so many fortunes. Art goes according to fashion, you know. Forty years ago you couldn't have given away a painting by one of the Pre-Raphaelites, and today they're out of sight. In about 1850, you could have picked up a Boucher, for instance, on the Continent for next to nothing.

"Well, George felt he had as good an eye as any expert for a fine work of art. He spent hours prowling around in antique shops and junk shops and he turned up Rubenses and van Dycks as well as the work of lesser masters—he had a Crome, a Teniers, and a Marieschi, for instance."

I said, "You're kidding! You mean this stuff was genuine?"

"I don't mean that at all, but George certainly thought so."

"Did he ever show any of it to an expert?"

"He had a rather unhappy experience with an expert quite a long time ago. He used to buy from a gallery in London, Pangloss, I suppose you've heard of them. No modern work, nothing later than the mid-nineteenth century. Well, a local chap, a small dealer in Minchinhampton, offered George a canvas, unsigned, which he said was by Fragonard. He wanted thirty quid for it, utterly absurd of course, but George said he wanted to take it home and live with it for a day or two. He took it to London instead, and showed it to his expert. Pangloss pooh-poohed it, said it was worthless. So George returned it. The fellow in Minchinhampton put it into a Christie's sale where it was catalogued not as a Fragonard, but as the work of Adrien Moreau, a nineteenth-century artist who occasionally imitated the style of the eighteenth century. It made over four hundred pounds."

"It's the kind of thing that can happen. Even experts make mistakes."

"Quite. Art experts, in my experience, are like doctors. Jolly good at preserving their air of infallibility, especially when they don't know what they're talking about. Most of us learn to be properly skeptical. But George felt he'd been let down. And he had been lucky several times, found rather nice little pictures in out-of-the-way places for reasonable prices. He was a stubborn sort of man. He felt that since he could trust his own judgment in business, why not in art? And so he went on finding Constables and Rembrandts at church bazaars and the like, buying them for five or ten pounds, having them cleaned, and proudly showing them off to his friends."

"Hm. Well, it's a harmless enough pastime. So when he died, I suppose he left nothing but junk. How come this little picture was sent to the auction?"

"Ah, well, he did actually have some very good things, most of them his earlier purchases from Pangloss. They were all sent to Sotheby's. The pictures Sotheby's wouldn't handle were given to the local auctioneers. There were fifteen of them at that sale, your copy among them."

I didn't like the way he stressed *copy* any more than I liked his hectoring air. On the other hand, everything about Puncheon rang all too familiar a bell. I knew people like that. And art experts could indeed be wrong. And within the last two years there had been several cases of first-rate paintings being bought from junk shops by enterprising amateurs. The whole thing made a convincing picture. It certainly explained how something like my little

41

landscape would belong to a wealthy collector. And if Sotheby's had rejected it that seemed to prove it was valueless.

But of course it wasn't valueless. It had gone to seventy pounds. And now Villiers was willing to swap a Rowlandson for it. I would have to give the matter a little thought.

I got up. "Well, thanks for the tea, Mrs. Villiers," I said. "I'd better be going."

"Here. Just a minute." Villiers rose, too. He was holding his voice down but his face was redder than it had been. "What about the picture?"

"I'll let you know," I said.

His wife said, with a laugh, "Have you been trying to get it away from Mr. Eddison, Charles?" And to me, "You mustn't let him bully you."

"That's enough," Villiers said. "Stay out of this."

She clamped her mouth shut but gave him a poisonous look.

He ignored it. "Look here," he said to me. "I've been more than fair, I think. I've been open with you. You can't just walk out without coming to a decision."

"Yes I can," I said.

He was growing angry. "I'm not having any of your dealer's tricks, damn it. Trying to push the price up, is that it?"

I stared at him. "Take it easy," I said, calmly. "I didn't ask you to buy anything. You've been chasing *me.*" My tone brought him up short. "I told you I'd get in touch with you. I'll let you have a yes or a no in a day or so. That's all I aim to do."

He stood motionless, and I could see uncertainty struggling in him with his natural bluster. I nodded to him and started for the door.

Mrs. Villiers came with me. "I'll show you out, Mr. Eddison," she said.

At the front door, she added, softly, "Don't mind Charles. He thinks of nothing but his collection. And you know how collectors are—like children. They'll go to any lengths to get something they've set their hearts on."

We shook hands and her hand was warm and clinging. "I do hope we'll have a chance to meet again," she said, giving me a look equally warm and clinging.

"I hope so," I replied, and I was careful to keep my voice courteous but noncommittal.

I found my way back to Altoncester without difficulty. I parked the car and went into the hotel, my mind still busy with Villiers, not at all sure yet what I'd do about his offer. As the man at the desk handed me my key, he said, "There's a young lady to see you, sir."

I was slow taking it in. Before I could ask him anything, somebody touched my arm.

It was Jill.

We put our arms around each other,
and I said, "What—?"

"Just a minute," she said, and kissed me. Then she said,
"Can't we go somewhere and talk?"

I took her up to my room in spite of the disapproving
looks we were getting from the man at the desk. We sat
down side by side on the flowered bedspread, holding
hands.

I had put everything out of my head except the fact that
she was there. Now I said, "All right. Let's have it."

"You mean, how I got here today instead of tomorrow?
I got permission to miss one session. And tonight there's
nothing but a sherry party with all the final post-mortem-
ing."

"I see. That isn't what I meant, though. Why didn't you
phone me last night?"

She laughed ruefully. "Oh, but I did. Two or three times.
Each time I got that whine that means the number is
unobtainable."

"But I wrote the number on the back of my telegram."

"Mm-hm. I began to feel sure that Aunt Grace had done
something wrong. I worried about you. I knew you were
here somewhere—she didn't know which hotel and wasn't
even sure which town you were in—but I knew you'd be
wondering why I hadn't phoned. That's why I had to come
back. She showed me the telegram. The number she had
given me was on the front, not the back. It turned out to
be the date."

44

"Oh, for Christ's sake! I knew it."

"Don't be too hard on her, poor dear. She did remember that there was a number and that it was on the telegram."

"All right. As long as you're here, now." I looked hungrily at her. "You've changed your hairdo. It's shorter."

"Do you like it?"

"I like everything about you. A whole year, Jill!"

"Oh, darling."

After a bit, I held her away and said, "Let's get married. Tomorrow."

Her eyes clouded. She held my face between her hands.

"Bob," she said, "I do love you. But I don't know what to decide."

I felt anger flame up in me.

"It's not easy for me," she went on. "Don't put on that stony look. I can't leave Aunt Grace. You know what she's like."

"We've been over all this before. She can manage. She's not all that helpless."

"It's not a matter of her being helpless. It's loneliness. She's not able to live alone. And there's my work—"

"You could teach in Connecticut. There are plenty of backward kids there."

"It's the children *here* I'm thinking of. I'm English, Bob. I'm concerned about English children."

I pulled away from her and stood up.

"Well, you're going to have to decide between your concern for them and your concern for me."

"You know it's not as simple as that. It's not just the children. Not just Aunt Grace, either."

"I know. It's pulling up stakes and going off to another country. You've said it before. I haven't forgotten."

"You haven't helped," she said, sadly. "You've written to me how dreadful things are over there in the States. The violence, the ugliness, the hatred—and with every letter my heart sank."

"You talk as if there were nothing wrong with England."

"Of course there are things wrong here. But it's my place. My family have lived in this part of Gloucestershire for centuries. Aunt Grace's house has belonged to the family since it was built, more than four hundred years ago. It's not easy to make up my mind to leave."

"Not even for me."

"Not even for you, Bob."

The water welled up in her eyes and a tear fell glittering. I felt a pang of tenderness for her, but it didn't help all that much.

I said, roughly, "Then that's the end of it."

"Ah, no," she cried. She sprang to her feet and came close to me. "Wait. Don't say it. You're going to say something you'll wish you could take back. Do you want me to go with you against my will?"

She held me by the jacket with one hand and with the back of the other smeared away the tears, like a child.

"I've come all this way," I began, and then couldn't go on.

"I know," she said. "I know. I've tried to think what to tell you ever since I knew you were here. I've rehearsed it a hundred different ways. I'm so confused."

She rested her forehead against my chest, wearily.

All my rage evaporated. I said, "Jill, it's no good. We can't keep this up, my seeing you once a year maybe, writing to each other, sending each other love and kisses. What's the sense of it? We're just tormenting each other."

She uttered a long sigh. "Give me a few days," she said.

"What for? What good will it do?"

"I don't know whether it will do any good. Seeing you suddenly this way changes things." She took out her handkerchief and blew her nose. "Let me talk to Aunt Grace," she said. "And to—you won't laugh?—to the vicar. He's known me ever since I was a little girl. But most of all, I just want to think. Now that you're actually here

46

everything's urgent. I will decide. I'll say yes or no, I promise you. Could you wait for two or three days?"

"All right," I said. "I'll wait three days. Okay? Give me a kiss."

She did. I murmured in her ear, "Stay here tonight."

She shook her head. "It'll just make it harder for me to make up my mind."

"I don't care."

"Yes, you do. It's not as if we hadn't ever slept together."

"That was a long time ago."

"No, darling. Let me go. It isn't that I don't want to stay. I'm afraid to."

"Oh, hell," I said. "At least have dinner with me."

She laughed in spite of herself, and so did I. "Just let me fix my face," she said.

It was past seven by then, and we went out to a restaurant she knew in the market square. We were both drained, and we had a drink, and ordered, and then sat looking at each other in silence for a few minutes.

"What will you do?" she said, rather timidly. "Stay in Altoncester?"

"I don't know. Maybe." I remembered that attractive village I'd driven through behind Villiers. "Do you know a place called Chaworth?"

"Oh, yes. It's charming. I hope it stays that way."

"Why?"

"There was some talk about quarrying limestone near the village. I have a friend who is a member of the CPRE here in Altoncester, and she says they have had quite a fight on their hands."

"What's the CPRE?"

"The Council for the Protection of Rural England. She told me that they had an inquiry pending over the matter. If it had gone through, this limestone quarry, there'd be dust and noise, and lorries roaring through the place—it

47

would be horrible. A man named Puncheon had something to do with it, owned the land and wanted to make it into a quarry."

"Puncheon? I heard that name just this afternoon. I wonder if it's the same man. The one I heard about is dead."

"That's right. It was in all the papers. He was murdered."

"Really?"

"By skinheads. At least, that's what everyone thinks although I don't think there was enough evidence for the police to arrest anyone."

"Skinheads—some kind of teenage gangs, aren't they? I've read something about them. I thought they were only in London or other big cities."

"There are some in almost every largish town. There are some in Altoncester. They cut their hair very short—what we used to think of as American style—"

"Crew cut."

"Yes, I suppose so. In distinction to the hippy types who let their hair grow long. Hence, skinheads. They wear thick boots and their speciality is knocking down and kicking. They call it 'stomping.' They started in cities like Manchester and Birmingham, mainly against the Pakistanis and Jamaicans who have been settling there. But the uniform and style have spread, the way being a Mod or a Rocker spread some years ago."

"And now they go for anybody, is that it? How'd they come to pick on this man Puncheon?"

"I don't actually know. It happened somewhere near Chaworth—"

"Is that where Puncheon lived?"

"Yes. He owned a large estate there, and a good deal of land. All I can remember is that the boys are said to have attacked him at night. I don't know what they could have been doing in Chaworth. There was something odd about his death, but I'm foggy about it. It happened some time ago, mind you, in March, I think. How did you happen to hear of him?"

I told her about my meeting with Villiers.

"I never heard of him," she said. "But I don't know many people in Chaworth."

"Well," I said, "I'd like to find out some more about this picture. It would be interesting to know where Puncheon got it, and what he thought about it. But I can't ask him."

"Maybe his wife would know," Jill said.

"Did he have a wife?"

"Oh, yes. Oddly enough, she's a member of CPRE, the very organization that was fighting her husband over the limestone quarry."

"The right hand not knowing what the left hand is doing? Or maybe she felt guilty. Well, it's an idea—maybe I could go to see her."

"Why don't you, darling?"

"It'll give me something to keep me busy, is that it?" I couldn't help grinning at her, and she flushed. "All right. There's a nice-looking hotel in Chaworth, the King's Head. I'll call them tomorrow and see if I can get a room. If I have to hang around for three days I'd rather be up there in that pretty village than down here in the town. And if you're right and they're going to wreck the place, I may as well see it before it vanishes."

We had finished our coffee. She said, "That's where you'll be, then?"

"Unless you hear otherwise from me. Are you going home now?"

"I think I'd better. I drove up from Sussex this afternoon, and I had classes before then from nine."

I leaned across the table towards her. "Jill," I said, "there's one thing. It probably doesn't mean anything but I have to ask you. We haven't talked about this, not really—I've had affairs with girls in the past and they never came to much, partly because I'm an Indian."

49

"I don't understand."

"It wasn't their fault. It was mine. Do you know how I think of you? I think of you as white."

"Oh," she said. "But darling, that's you. What's it got to do with me?"

"Are you sure that somewhere in your mind there isn't a little of that kind of thinking? Is it possible that my color's one of the reasons you can't make up your mind?"

She put her hands over mine. "I'm sure it isn't. I love your color. I'd be lying if I said I never think of you as an Indian. But when I do, I do so with pride. I've been reading everything I could get from the library about the Cherokees. They were a great people."

She smiled, her eyes crinkling in the particularly merry way that was hers. "I'd have said," she added, "that being a Cherokee was very nearly as good as being an Englishman."

I walked her to her rattly old Mini and we stood beside it for a last embrace. "Will I see you before the three days are up?" I asked.

"I don't know. I shouldn't wonder. Let's see. And darling, don't offer me any more obstacles than I already have."

"I understand, Jill."

She drove off and I felt lonelier than I had any time during the past year.

I was able to reserve a room in the King's Head next morning and I drove to Chaworth after breakfast. The hotel was managed by an elderly woman, very straight-backed and military. She introduced herself as Mrs. Orchard and told me that she hoped I'd be comfortable; the way she put it it sounded like an order. I asked her where I could find Mrs. Puncheon. "At home, I should have thought," she replied, sternly, plunking a local telephone book down before me.

Mrs. Puncheon agreed to see me that morning, and Mrs.

Orchard, when I asked her for directions, summoned me to her Regimental HQ and gave me an Ordnance Survey map of the area. With it open on the front seat, I took the route out of the village along which I'd gone with Villiers. The way led past his road, however, and on for another quarter of a mile or so to a crossroads. Common land stretched around me, open and grassy. To the left, the ground dropped a little and rose again like an ocean swell, and I could see the road running across it to a ragged heap of gray stone. According to my map this was the ruin of a castle. To the right, the road dipped into the dark foliage of oaks and beeches which encroached on the Common. I took that way. Shortly, I found myself driving along a high stone wall. This was Chaworth Court. I turned in past a gatehouse and up a short drive to a large, handsome house of Cotswold stone, square built, with long windows, dignified and vaguely French.

A maid in an apron answered my knock, and led me into a sunny south-facing room where a tall, white-haired woman rose from a desk to greet me.

"How do you do, Mr. Eddison," she said. "I am Julia Puncheon. Won't you sit down?"

I suppose it can hardly be accidental that so many upperclass English people resemble horses, considering the long association between the two races. Mrs. Puncheon had a long bony face, nervous nostrils, large teeth, and lustrous but rather stupid eyes. Her voice was high and whinnying. Around her neck was a trapping of heavy gold chains that jingled when she moved like horse-brasses. I restrained myself from patting her on the back.

"I gather from your telephone conversation," she said, "that you are interested in my late husband's art collection. I'm afraid the paintings have been sold, but I still have a few pieces of sculpture. Would you like to see them?"

"Perhaps later, Mrs. Puncheon," I said. "Right now, I'm

51

more interested in this." I had brought the painting, and I unwrapped it and showed it to her.

"Ah, yes," she said, rearing back to look at it with equine myopia. "I remember it. It's the one Charles liked so much. Have you bought it?"

"Yes," I said. "By Charles do you mean Charles Villiers?"

"That's right. Do you know him?"

"We've met. Can you tell me anything about this picture, Mrs. Puncheon?"

"What would you like to know? I'm afraid I'm not very knowledgeable about art."

"Anything you can tell me. I'd be very grateful."

I gave her my rare, shy smile with the dazzling teeth against the bronzed skin, the captivating rustic lad smile. Oddly enough, it seemed to affect her. She smiled back as if I were offering her an apple.

"Well," she said, "you see, when my husband died I wondered what to do with all the things he'd bought. I was certain some of them must be worth quite a lot of money. Then when Charles came along to see me I asked his opinion."

"About what to do with them?"

"Yes. He wanted to buy that picture, you see."

"Why didn't you sell it to him?"

"As I say, Mr. Eddison, I know very little about art." She gave me a sidelong look. "I do know something about collectors, however. My husband was one, an inveterate one. And Charles collects, too. I thought it might be wise to have some sort of objective opinion about, well, values, before plunging into anything, do you see?"

I saw, all right. A collector naturally always offers the lowest possible figure. I saw, too, that Mrs. Puncheon was a lot smarter than any horse.

She went on, "Charles was very agreeable and helpful, I must say. He offered to take all the paintings to Sotheby's for me."

52

"That must have been difficult," I said. "Why didn't you just have one of their appraisers come here?"

"I'd have had to pay his fare and his fee," she said, with all the candor of someone rich enough to pinch pennies. "In any case, they are apparently reluctant to send anyone unless it's a matter of something really grand. I loaned Charles our estate car and he drove to London one day. I think he knows someone at Sotheby's—he goes to the sales quite often. Well, then, Sotheby's took twenty-six pictures they thought they could do quite well with, and rejected fourteen or fifteen, which Charles brought back. I decided to put those into our local sale, through Craig and Locke."

"Very wise of you," I said. "Do you mind my asking you something which may sound impertinent? How much did Mr. Villiers offer you for the little landscape, back at the start?"

"Ten pounds," she said, with a smile.

She had done well to be cautious of collectors.

I said, "This is all very interesting, Mrs. Puncheon. Have you any idea where your husband bought this picture?"

"I really can't say. He used to visit the local antique shops regularly, and he had all sorts of connections with dealers in various villages or towns like Bristol and Bath. Oh, I know," she added, "you might ask Sir Donald Sterlet. George trusted his taste and knowledge, and often brought pictures to him for an opinion. Sometimes Donald went with him on his buying expeditions. He might be able to tell you what you want to know."

"Great. Does Sir Donald live here in Chaworth?"

"Oh, yes. He lives in a house called Pellet Lane on the far side of the village. Anyone can show it to you." She hesitated, and then said, "I should warn you, Donald is rather odd. But perhaps, being an American, you won't find him so."

I grinned. I had met one or two eccentric English people and I thought I could visualize this old boy; he probably kept lions in the garden or grew giant aspidistras.

I said, "Thank you very much. You've been very help-ful."

"Would you like to look at the sculpture?" she asked.

"Sure, why not?" I said.

She took me across the hall into an imposing library where, in addition to shelves of books from floor to ceiling, there was plenty of room for a life-sized marble nymph, a four-foot-high gilded bronze boddhisatva, and one or two other monstrous pieces.

"I'm afraid they aren't for me," I said.

She sighed. "I didn't really think they would be," she admitted. "My husband often bought things because he thought them a good investment. Art and—a great many other things as well. But these are really rather hideous." She sighed again, nodding at the nymph. "He bought that only a few days before his death. He was certain it was very ancient, Roman or Greek or something of the sort. I suspect he was wrong."

"I heard about what happened to him. Some kids did it, didn't they? I didn't realize you had that kind of violence over here."

"It was monstrous. Shocking. The wretched boys had been coming up from Altoncester to one of our pubs, to drink. They'd been in several brawls. My husband was out one night on business and they caught him alone. Why they should have wanted to harm him I can't imagine. I don't believe he had ever even seen them before."

"That's the way these young hoods are," I said. "They'll gang up on somebody just for the hell of it. Maybe your husband said something that annoyed them."

"It is possible," Mrs. Puncheon said, drily. "He often said things that annoyed people. Oh, don't misunderstand me. He wasn't a quarrelsome man. Nor did he have many enemies. He had a few opponents—it's hardly possible to try to benefit people without stepping on one or two toes.

But he was always working for the good of the community as he saw it. He donated a lot of money to the building of the youth center. He repaired and rebuilt the cottages of all our tenants and never charged them a penny more in rent. He was active on several committees, and he was responsible for having the fine old Market House repaired. All sorts of things. He was the last person you'd expect to be involved in a fight with—with—"

Her voice faltered. "I'm sorry," she said. "I don't like talking about it. I can't understand it, and never shall."

I murmured something sympathetic, and we went back to the drawing room so I could rewrap my picture. As I was doing so, I caught sight of a silver-framed photograph of a man on a desk against the wall. He had a heavy, flabby face, but the pouchy eyes were full of humor and there was the ghost of a smile of great self-contentment on the puffy lips. He looked like a man who had no reason to find fault with himself.

Mrs. Puncheon saw me looking and said, "That was my husband."

I said, "Thank you again. May I ask a favor? If anything should occur to you, I mean if you find out anything more about where or how your husband got this painting, or even how much he paid for it, I'd appreciate it if you'd get in touch with me. I'm staying at the King's Head and I should be there for another couple of days at least. Will you do that?"

I gave her another smile, one of my best, and she said that she would. She saw me to the door. I got into my car and started off to find Sir Donald Sterlet.

I couldn't help thinking as I drove how even more curious all this was. Mrs. Puncheon had told me how much good her husband had done for the community and how everybody loved him, and yet she herself, according to Jill, had been a member of the very organization that had been opposing him. Still, it was none of my business. All I wanted to do now was settle for myself what was rapidly becoming an obsession: the history of a painting which was worthless and which had nevertheless brought $170 at auction.

Driving back through Chaworth, I was struck again by its qualities. It wasn't just a pretty postcard but a living place, busy but quiet, handsome but not self-conscious. Its beauties of stone and wood, gardens and vines, had grown up out of the centuries and I felt that each person who had built there had done so with a certain pride in his own house and in the village to which he was adding. The band of modern cottages stood out against this background even more exceptionally; they had been thrown up for quick money, and it showed. I thought of Altoncester with its streets jammed by traffic, its old bones rattling to the passage of giant trailers, its air stinking and noisy, and whatever had once been good to look at walled up and plastered over by commercialism. I was puzzled by what I knew of George Puncheon. How could a man work, as his wife had said, for the good of the community and yet be willing to toss it to the disasters of a limestone quarry?

A man in a long white coat unloading a butcher's van gave me directions. I had to turn down a narrow side street and at the edge of the village, where there was a small pub and a cottage where honey and eggs were sold, leave my car and walk between hedges to a pair of rusty iron gates that hung permanently open. The name *Pellet Lane* was cut into the stone of one of the gateposts.

The house looked to have been put up in about 1600 and to have been falling down ever since. Most of its windows were broken. Part of the roof was gone and moss and weeds grew from the cracked rim. The couple of steps leading up to the front door had collapsed into rubble, and a large fungus, like an ominous piece of liver, grew out of the doorjamb itself. It didn't seem possible that anyone had lived here since Count Dracula had vacated it.

I started walking around towards the back. There was a path through the shrubbery, overgrown with weeds sprouting through a crust of unraked leaves. It led me to a wall in which there was an opening with hinges, but no door. I stepped through into a paved courtyard. There was a stone outbuilding which had once been a stable, and in front of it signs of life: a small garbage can overflowing with empty tins, eggshells, and mouldy bread at which a sparrow was pecking. A flight of steps, or rather a shamble of steps, staggered up the outside wall to a door at the top, and from somewhere up there I could hear a voice monotonously cursing.

I mounted cautiously because I wasn't positive the stairs would hold. Up above, I could make out that it wasn't cursing I heard but singing, a very discordant and emphatic singing:

> "Gloria in excelsis Deo
> And the same to you."

Whoever it was sang in a hoarse tenor, to the tune of "Onward Christian Soldiers."

I knocked. After a couple of minutes, the door was flung open. A man in his early thirties stood blinking at me. He was fair-haired, fair-bearded, glassy-eyed. His hair and beard had bits of fluff in them and his shirt and jeans were equally dirty, so that he looked as if someone had used him to dust out a room.

"Who the hell are you?" he asked.

I said, "My name's Eddison."

"Oh, yes. I know. The inventor of electricity."

"I'm looking for Sir Donald Sterlet."

"You are, eh? What for? Want to read the meter?"

"Are you Sir Donald?"

"I'm Sir bloody Donald, but don't ask me to prove it. And who are you? No, that's right, I remember, I saw you in the films inventing the gramophone."

"Can I come in?"

"Come in, dear boy. Come in, come in, come in."

He moved back, almost falling. There was one big room and it was surprisingly light because a long window had been inserted into the rear wall, which faced south. There was an unmade bed covered with odds and ends of clothing, a kitchen chair, an easel, and not much else in the way of furniture. Cans of paint stood about on the paint-splattered floor. Brushes and tubes of color were mingled with greasy plates, cups, and big brown bottles of West Country cider. There was a dirty sink in one corner and a small gas stove. His palette was a sheet of glass balanced on two upended wooden boxes, and there were canvases stacked along the walls and one on the easel at which he had been working.

I glanced at it. It was a strange and striking composition, a dream city hanging in the air above pale, watery fields, with people fishing from its edges for birds. The nearest I can come to describing it is to say that it reminded me vaguely of some of Paul Klee's early work, but only vaguely; it was deeply and distinctively original.

I said, "I like that."

He chuckled. "You like it, do you? That's damned decent of you. And I am grateful, old boy. By God, I'm bloody grateful. Would you like me to kiss your arse or perform some other act of humility?"

His tone, however, was not really hostile. So I laughed and said, "Okay. You win. What I should have said is that I think it's a hell of a good picture. That's the truth."

He picked up one of the bottles and thoughtfully drank from it. He offered it to me and I wiped the neck and tried it. It wasn't what we call cider, which is sweet apple juice, but the strong English country stuff, which is as potent as moonshine.

"You're right, you know," he said. "For an electrician you show surprising taste. It's a bloody marvelous picture. Just think what it'll be like when I've finished with it."

"Who handles your stuff?" I asked.

"Who?" he said, uncertainly. "Oh, I've tried London once or twice. But they've got no time for a rustic like me. A muddy-booted boor," he said, savoring the words. It was surprising how clear his speech was, considering the load he must have been carrying. "A hempen homespun. It's not so easy to get a gallery. Too much art and too few patrons. I've sold a few pictures through a nice friendly chap in Bristol. But you see, I'm a slow worker. That thing—" he thrust his chin at the easel, "I've been more than a fortnight fooling about with it. I don't know how much longer it'll take. And if I get fifty nicker for it I'll be lucky. People hereabouts don't want to pay much, not unless they can feel they're getting an investment."

He looked warily at me. "Are you a Canadian?"

"I'm an American."

"I never can tell the difference. Don't tell me you came here to buy something."

"I don't know. I'd like to see some more of your stuff. But actually, I came to ask you something."

"Ask away," he said. "Accept the hospitality of my house. I'm sorry we can't go into the great drawing room but there are bats in it. The bedrooms are similarly occupied by spiders and other creepy-crawlies. You'd never guess what a pleasant place this was when I was a kid. However, you can have the chair. Do sit down, Mr. Eddison. As for me, I'll stand."

He then lowered himself heavily to the floor and sipped from his bottle. "What d'you want to ask?" he said.

I began unwrapping the painting. "I bought this at an auction in Altoncester," I explained. "I'd like to find out some more about it, if I can. You see, I'm a dealer in Connecticut. I expect to sell it. Obviously, if I knew some more about where it came from, something about who painted it, how much it cost—anything like that—it would be a help."

He laid aside his refreshment, wiped his hands on his shirt, and took the painting. He gazed at it for a while, swaying slightly, and then said, "I've seen this before, haven't I?"

"I don't know," I said. "You tell me. I know it belonged to a man named George Puncheon. His wife couldn't tell me anything about it but she said you were a friend of his and sometimes advised him about purchases."

He broke into laughter. "A friend of his?" he said. "That's bloody marvelous. I didn't know the bastard had any friends."

I said, in surprise, "I thought he was a kind of public benefactor."

"Let me tell you something about public benefactors, dear boy," said Sterlet. "They exist in their own minds. Is that what I mean? What I mean is, they never stop to think whether the public wants their bloody benefactions. They say, 'Right, chums, I'll put up a statue here to Lord Palmerston with a drinking trough for oxen, or maybe a public refuge for anti-blood-sport people who are being pursued by Hunt members,' and they go ahead and spend a bloody fortune on it. But who needs it? Not the public, who never heard of Lord bloody Palmerston and don't give a damn about either the Hunt or the anti-blood-sport people. But it looks well in the obituary notices: 'Among his many civic works were. . . .'

"Now you take George Puncheon. He's been living in Chaworth for fifteen years or so, ever since he married my cousin Julia. He has striven to do nothing but good among us, lumpy proletarians though we are. Restored the old Market Hall and got himself made chairman of the parish council, a strategic position. And while he has led committees in the fight for local improvement, he has been buying land all over the place. In response to Britain's housing shortage he put up fifty cottages on the northern edge of the village. I believe he made a packet from that

61

operation. Whatever he did, he rarely forgot to make a profit."

"His wife said he repaired their tenants' houses free."

"Why not? That came under the heading of property improvement. He was a kindly man. He has even allowed me to live here at a nominal rental, a pound a month."

"Here? I thought this house belonged to you."

"It did, old boy, it did. Or rather, to my family. My father was an adequate baronet but a rotten businessman. After the war things were pretty bad and they got worse. My mother died when I was about twelve and after that he didn't seem to care about much. The house was going to ruin and he couldn't afford to have it repaired, and didn't give a damn anyway. We lived in two rooms. I'd come home for the holidays—he managed to keep me in school —and he'd spend the time walking with me but saying nothing, or sitting and staring at the wall. About ten years ago he sold the house to Puncheon, keeping the right to live on in it for the rest of his life. That wasn't long. He hanged himself a year later."

"That's tough," I said.

Sterlet shrugged. "Poor old chap, the world had changed out of all recognition for him. It wasn't just my mother's death. England was different, far too different. The world he grew up in was rather jolly, and it all blew up when the first bombs fell. He couldn't cope. He wasn't much of a coper. He couldn't cope with me, either. I can see how I must have been a hell of a disappointment to him."

He was still holding my picture and he nodded at it with a wry grin. "This sort of stuff, you know. Mucking about with paint. It was absolutely impenetrable for him, and so was I."

Abruptly, he held the picture out to me. "Here. I'm afraid there's nothing I can tell you about it," he said.

"You haven't any idea where Puncheon might have bought it?"

"He bought things from all sorts of shady dens. He was always trying to pick up bargains."

"And you did sometimes go with him and give him advice?"

"Why not? He always stood me drinks. Sometimes, if I was particularly charming, lunch as well. He'd show me some Victorian daub and ask whether I thought it could be by Constable and I'd have to explain that it couldn't. Sometimes, he'd buy it anyway. But now and then he'd turn up a landscape, say, by one of those hard-working sods who painted cows in the best R.A. style, and then I could give an opinion."

I said, "I see. When I first showed this to you you said you'd seen it before. What about that?"

He rubbed a hand across his chin, leaving a faint smear of blue paint. "Did I?" he said. "I don't think so. I'm sure I didn't. I've seen so many loathsome pictures it's hard for me to tell."

"Then you never saw this one?"

He shook his head. I was puzzled. I could have sworn he was lying, but I couldn't imagine why he should be. I tried to remember exactly what he had said, but I couldn't.

"Well," I said, "now that you've seen it, what do you think of it?"

"I never give free opinions. Buy me a drink?"

"Any time you say."

"I say now."

"Fine."

He got himself up off the floor and scrabbled around amongst the mess on his bed until he found an elbowless cardigan, which he put on.

"I'll give you my authoritative appraisal first," he said, "and then we'll go down to the Fleece."

He took the picture from me again. He picked his way among the cans and junk on the floor, going over to the window, and on the way he slipped and nearly fell as his foot came down on a steel ball which had been lying on the floor, a sort of oversized marble. It rolled off and I caught his arm, fearful he'd drop the picture.

"I'm all right," he said, pulling away. He studied the

painting for a time in the light, and then said, "I think it's a right 'un."

"What do you mean, a right 'un?"

"I mean I think it was done by a real painter. No bloody amateur did that."

"Hm. Would you say it was Dutch?"

"Maybe. Might even be early."

I took it back and turned it over. "Did you ever hear of H. T. Maxwell?"

"Who's he?"

I showed him the paper pasted on the back. He began to laugh.

"What's so funny?" I said.

"It shows you how wrong I can be. Still, it's a damned good copy, isn't it?"

"Yes," I said, "I think so. Of course, I've never seen the original. Is it possible Maxwell was a professional artist?"

"Oh, no doubt of it. I never heard of him but that doesn't mean a thing. There were hundreds of solid professionals in the last part of that century. He needn't have been an English academician. He might have been a Scot. Or even an American, who traveled over here."

"That's true. I never thought of that."

"While you're thinking, what about that drink?"

We started to go, and I said, "Hold on a second. I'd like to look at some of your paintings."

That stopped him. "You're serious, aren't you?" he said.

"That's right."

"I only have half a dozen finished pictures here." He pulled some of the canvases away from the wall and turned them to the light.

They were all in the same vein as the unfinished one on the easel, strikingly imaginative, informed with wit, their weird shapes charged with energy. There was no question of his talent.

I particularly liked one small one, organized around a

luminous birdlike form among calligraphic shapes which I took to be branches, or messages in bird-script.

"How much do you want for that?" I asked.

"I really don't know," he said. "I hadn't given it any thought. Are you very rich?"

"No. You tell me what you want and I'll tell you whether I can afford it."

"Twenty pounds?"

That was fifty dollars. Not much to pay for a painting. I felt a twinge of guilt; I knew I was getting it cheaply and I had paid considerably more than that for the landscape by a man who was long dead and couldn't benefit.

"I guess I can afford it," I said. "Look, I'll tell you what we'll do. Let's go have a beer together, or whatever you want. Then I'll get some cash and you meet me at the King's Head at seven. Wrap the picture for me and bring it along, and I'll pay you then. If you're free we'll have dinner together. How's that?"

He looked at me with approval. "I'd like that."

We clambered down the stairs. At the bottom, Sterlet straightened, drew a few long breaths, and at once appeared to be sober. As we were going out between the iron gates, I said, "I'm curious about the name of the house. What's it mean?"

"Pellet Lane? How's your French?"

"What's my French got to do with it?"

"The place was built in the 1590s by a wool merchant. He brought over a number of Huguenot weavers, and gave the house a French name to celebrate his profits: *Pelote de Laine,* a sharp old chap. Too bad I haven't inherited any of his business sense."

I looked back at the place. "How come Puncheon never repaired it if he was so fond of property values?"

"Oh, he wanted it to go on dropping to bits. That was part of his strategy. You see, there's some kind of hard limestone under here, very suitable for road stone. His aim was to demolish the place eventually and start quarrying. I told you, he always had an eye on profit. He had a lot more in common with my ancestor old *Pelote de Laine* than I have."

"I heard about the quarry," I said. "So you have a reprieve now?"

"Maybe. I don't know what's going to happen."

We walked down the lane to the pub where I had parked. Over its door was a faded sign, a sheep hanging from a ribbon: The Fleece. We went into the public bar.

The man behind the counter, a meaty-looking bruiser with a few strands of hair combed wetly across his pink scalp, said, "All right, then, Sir Donald?"

"Pretty middling, Jack," Sterlet said. I had once had it explained to me that in Gloucestershire that meant "pretty well," while "very middling" meant "pretty bad."

I said, "What'll you drink? Beer?"

"God, yes. The muck I've been drinking tastes like chobblings." He grinned at me. "There's a good word for you. When rats nibble at your apples and leave pulpy crumbs, those are chobblings."

"A descriptive language."

"If you want to hear really descriptive language," Sterlet said, "you should listen to Jack, here, dealing with the skinheads who come to us from Altoncester."

"Ar. They'm a shiftless lot," Jack said, contemptuously.

He drew two pints of the local bitter with care and set them before us. At my suggestion he drew a third for himself, thanked me gravely, and tasted it.

"These kids from Altoncester," I said. "I heard that some of them murdered Mr. Puncheon."

The publican gave me a suspicious look and then glanced at Sterlet. Sterlet laughed.

"No, you needn't bridle, Jack," he said. "This gentleman has come all the way from America to buy one of my paintings, so you ought to be as civil as possible to him."

"Any friend o' yourn, then, Sir Donald," said Jack.

Sterlet went on, to me, "Yes, that was what we heard. It seems to have begun when a gang of them were here the night before George was killed. They got rather rowdy and made the mistake of trying to push one of our neighbors around, a sweet old man, Mr. Mirkshot. We handled them roughly, I'm afraid."

The publican uttered a growling chuckle. "There's chap as did most of the handling, see," he said, with a nod.

I looked behind me, and for the first time saw a man sitting in a shadowy corner of the room. He was so still as to be little more than a shadow himself. An empty glass stood on the table before him, and in answer to Jack he raised it in a silent salute.

"Come and join us, William," said Sterlet. "My American friend is going to pay me a vast sum of money for a painting. We're celebrating."

The other got up and came so softly to the bar that it was as if some of the darkness had detached itself and floated towards us. He was a big man, not over tall but very bulky in the chest and shoulders, and thick in the middle. In spite of this barrel-shape he moved lightly. I've done considerable deer-hunting and I was willing to bet this fellow was a hunter.

He said, in a soft but carrying voice, "I can't make 'ead nor tail out'n they drawings o' yourn, my dear, but I'm 'appy to 'ear it. A brown ale, then, Jack. Thanking you, sir," he added to me.

Sterlet had finished his pint and I bought him another. He gulped at it and when he spoke again his speech was fuzzier.

"William picked up one of the boys, asked me politely to open the door, and threw him out into the road," he said, laughing. "Another of them, of the boys, jumped on his back and William picked him off as you might pick a straw off your shoulder. Assuming you had a straw, of course, on your shoulder. Oh, it was great fun. Before any of the rest of us could move, Jack came from behind the bar and said, 'Now, then.' Remember, Jack? 'Now, then, let's have no trouble, please.' One of the yobs swung at him and Jack knocked him clear across the room."

He became helpless with merriment, and drank the rest of his beer. "You don't mind paying for another, do you, dear boy?" he said. "You can deduct it from the twenty quid."

Jack said, "Now, Sir Donald—"

"Don't Sir Donald me and don't now me," Sterlet said. "You're worse than Mrs. Basket. What was I saying? Oh, yes, well after that little skirmish we thought we'd seen the last of them. But the very next night they seem to have returned. Looking for revenge, I suppose. At any rate that's when they did for George. But of course nothing was ever proved."

"What about a nice bit of bread and cheese, Sir Donald?" Jack said, coaxingly. "Or a nice pasty just come in fresh this morning?"

He looked at me and I could read the message in his eyes.

I said, "That's a great idea. I could do with something to eat. Let's have a couple of those pasties."

Sterlet had gone rather bleary. He blinked at me, and said, "All right, dear boy. Whatever you say. The thing I don't understand is what the hell George was doing there in the first place."

"Doing where?" I asked.

"At the castle. It's only a ruin. They've been restoring it, you know, getting it ready for the tourists this summer, but it isn't quite finished. It's a lovely spot. I walk there sometimes, and so does William. But then, we have our own reasons, don't we, William?"

The big man gazed at him. His silence, which had been the unobtrusiveness of a good stalker, suddenly became ominous.

"But nobody will ever know what George's reason was," Sterlet continued. He tapped me on the chest with a forefinger. "Let me tell you something. It was extraordinary, the way he was killed. When did those yobbos attack him? They came here in an old motor car. You could hear it popping and pooping a mile away. Somebody heard them drive up that night. But William was there and never heard a thing, did you, William? Bright moonlight, too, but he never saw a thing, either."

William moved in close, still without speaking. He loomed grimly at my right elbow. The publican had put a plate of meat pasties on the counter and he cleared his throat and said, softly, "Here we are, Sir Donald. A nice bite of lunch. There'll be some of the regulars coming in any minute, look. Whatever people think they saw or didn't see, why it's nobody's business but their own, now is it?"

I could feel the tension in the air around us, a tangible thing like a net that drew the four of us close. And then, as if emphasizing Jack's words, the door opened and a couple of men came into the bar.

"Afternoon, Jack."

"All right, then, Harold?"

"Bearing up."

William had vanished from beside me. Sterlet had bitten into one of the pasties and crumbs of meat and pastry showered down his shirt front. Jack was drawing neat pints. I was left feeling that I had fabricated any strain there was out of my own overactive imagination.

I left Sterlet beginning another pint and went to find a bank. The oddness of that few minutes had faded but from time to time puzzlement nudged me and I recalled Sterlet's words: *I walk there sometimes and so does William, but we have our own reasons. . .Extraordinary, the way he was killed. . . .*What had he been suggesting? And then I told myself again that the publican had had the right idea. It was none of my business. None of it except the Maxwell painting. I hadn't been such a fool about it after all, if a painter of Sterlet's abilities had taken it for seventeenth-century Dutch. Yet, in a way, that made the whole thing even more peculiar. Because, I told myself, just consider: Suppose I worked for a big auction house like Sotheby's and someone had brought a painting of this quality to me? Wouldn't I be tempted to remove the label from the back and catalogue it as a Dutch school painting? But no, perhaps not; perhaps they were as scrupulous as I was. Or on the other hand, perhaps they had seen some defect in it which neither Sterlet nor I could notice. Or—aha!—maybe the Sotheby's man knew the original from which this had been copied. That would explain everything.

I set it all aside for the time being. I had another painting to think about, and I had to get some cash for Sterlet. I searched my mind to see whether I regretted buying his picture. I have an infallible test for finding out whether I really want something; I ask myself whether I'd be upset if someone else nipped in and bought it from under my nose. In this case, the answer was yes, so I drove up to the high street of the village in search of a bank.

There was a branch of Barclay's, but it was only open on Tuesdays from ten to twelve. One more piece of English casualness, I fumed. However, it occurred to me that my hotel would probably cash a traveller's check.

Mrs. Orchard looked me up and down like a good commanding officer to make sure all my buttons were buttoned and then cashed a fifty-dollar check for me.

"There is a message for you," she added, and handed me a piece of paper. On it was written, *Mr. Villiers. Would like you to ring back.*

"When did he phone?" I asked.

Mrs. Orchard pointed severely to the slip and I saw that she had written 11:03 on it. I should have known better than to ask.

I got Villiers's number out of the book and dialled him.

"Ah, Mr. Eddison," he said, and I had to hold the receiver away from my ear. "Your hotel in Altoncester told me you'd moved to the King's Head. I'm delighted that you've decided to visit our village. I hope you're comfortable."

"Yes, thanks."

"Um—I very much regret the way we parted. I may have allowed my enthusiasm as a collector to carry me away. I'm sure with your experience you know how these things are."

"Uh-huh."

"You—ah—said you would give me an answer today. About our little swap, you know."

"What I said was in a day or so. The reason I haven't called you is that I still haven't made up my mind."

There was silence for a moment, then, "I see," he said. "Aren't you satisfied with my offer? I don't see how I could be fairer."

He sounded fretful. I said, "No, it isn't that. I'm not

71

satisfied with my information about the painting. I'm trying to find out a little more about it. I saw Mrs. Puncheon this morning—"

"Oh, did you?" he said.

"That's right."

"I doubt she told you very much. She isn't frightfully keen on paintings."

"No, not much."

"What, precisely, were you trying to find out, Mr. Eddison?" he said, belligerently.

"Oh, you know—just anything. For instance, it might be helpful if I knew where Puncheon bought the picture." And I added, "I don't suppose you know, do you?"

He chuckled. "As a matter of fact, I do," he said, giving me the surprise of the morning. I would have been willing to bet that if he knew, he'd never tell me.

As if he guessed what I was thinking, he said, "There isn't much to be learned about the provenance of that picture. I've already investigated. It belonged to an old woman, the granddaughter of H. T. Maxwell, the man who painted it. She sold it to the dealer who sold it to George."

"Oh," I said.

A tinge of skepticism must have colored my tone, because he uttered another hearty ha-ha and said, "I imagine you'd like to be convinced, wouldn't you?"

"Well, yes, I would."

"Let me ask you something. Supposing I could put you in touch with the dealer in question. I think he could quickly satisfy you. Would you then be interested in my offer?"

"I might. I'd be a lot more interested than I am now."

"Good enough. Give me a few minutes on the blower and I'll see what I can do. I'll ring you back."

He hung up, leaving me thoughtful.

He phoned in ten minutes or so. "A slight problem," he said. "Thompson—that's the chap's name—is going to be

72

tied up all afternoon. However, he can meet you tonight."

"Okay. Where? Here at the hotel?"

"No. No, that won't do," he said. There was a peculiar note in his voice, an unusual uncertainty. "I—ah—I haven't been altogether candid with you, Mr. Eddison."

"Is that so?"

"I'm rather embarrassed about this. Perhaps I should have mentioned it before. But it wasn't until I talked to him that I discovered—you see, he's—mm—he's being watched by the police."

"You mean he's a crook?"

"He's not as honest as he might be. I'm afraid he sometimes mixes himself up in rather shady affairs. It's no secret to me, of course. Nor was it to George. One sometimes—ah—"

He trailed off but I knew what he meant. One sometimes gets hold of good bargains if they're too hot for the general market.

"He was very open about it with me," he went on, after a moment. "He said, 'If your friend comes to my shop, or I go to his hotel, he may get into trouble.' "

"He's right, I guess. So that kills it, eh?"

"Oh, no. You could meet by accident. If you were to go to a certain pub in Altoncester—his local, you understand—you could quite accidentally fall into conversation with him. He feels certain the police don't pay much attention to him when he goes there."

"That's reasonable."

"Just so. They'd be watching anyone who came to his house, or marking anyone he paid a special visit to. But this way, it could all look quite casual. You'd drop in for a drink, fall into talk with him, show him the painting and he'd tell you all about it."

"All right," I said. "What's the pub called?"

"The Trumpet. It's in Brewers Lane, at the south edge of town. Do you know Altoncester?"

73

"Not too well, but I'll find the place. What time?"

"About nine-thirty, I should think. You go into the lounge bar, which should be fairly empty, and try to find a corner seat. I've described you to him, and in any case if you're carrying the picture that'll identify you."

"Then he'll make contact with me, is that it?"

"Yes, not to worry. All right?"

"If it works, it's all right."

"And you'll ring me in the morning and tell me how you got on?"

"I'll do that."

"Excellent. Goodbye, then, until tomorrow."

I looked forward to meeting Mr. Thompson. I knew dealers of his sort, some of them very knowledgeable men who had connections with rich collectors or museums that didn't mind where their goods came from. They were apt to be racy types, living more dangerously than the rest of us humdrum dealers, and their perspective about works of art or antiques was quite different: they handled pieces of property. It would be interesting talking to him, but it would be equally interesting to see if I could figure out whether he was telling the truth or only repeating a lie for which Villiers might have paid him. I thought that with the right questions, and as one dealer to another, I could find out.

Meanwhile, I had the afternoon on my hands and there was no word from Jill. I wondered whether she was in school in Altoncester right now, and whether I could find the place and stare at her through the window. I put the temptation out of my head. The day was fair, one of those June days of high-massed cloud and passages of sun, and I decided to explore the countryside.

Mrs. Orchard loaned me a guide book and I began by looking up Chaworth. "An attractive village, perched on the hills above the River Leach with extensive views westward and southward, its name is taken from its association with Payne de Chaworth, one of the Marcher lords whose holdings, as well as lands in Gloucestershire, included the Welsh fief of Kidwelly. Chaworth castle, originally no more than a keep protecting the heights, was enlarged in the 13th century, at which time, presumably, the hamlet grew up around it. Its seneschal was Bogo de Hacche, a noted warrior, whose family held the castle for the Chaworths until the 15th century. During the Civil Wars, the explosion of a quantity of gunpowder stored in a guard room caused considerable damage. After the wars its walls were thrown down and it ceased to be inhabited. Some of the stones were used in the repair of buildings in the village. The village itself contains many good examples of 17th and 18th century houses, and an arcaded market hall. The church, which miraculously evaded the savage hands of Puritan soldiers and 19th century restorers alike, is mainly EE and contains some good brasses."

I decided to start with the castle. It was a short drive to the crossroads where I'd been earlier. This time I turned to the left, following the smooth rise of the ground to the crest where the ruins stood. There were a couple of other cars near the walls and I parked and got out.

This was all common land and the grass was cropped short by the commoners' horses and cattle. It was springy underfoot, a thick-piled carpet figure with tiny daisies and dandelions. The air was buoyant and clear, more invigorating than the common element; it seemed to lighten you to the ends of the fingers with each breath you drew. Fleeces of cloud moved languidly across the sky and at the height where I stood they seemed lower than usual, so that I looked across, rather than up, at them. Away to the west and south lay the valleys patched with fields or clumps of woodland, and in the distance I could see the rippling line of the Welsh mountains, blue and misty. The quiet was reinforced, rather than broken, by the sound of a hammer on stone somewhere, and suddenly a lark sprang up and fluttered, trilling, over my head. It was a place to wash away all stress and I stood there for a long time, drawing deep breaths, before I wanted to move.

And then I reminded myself that it was also the place where a man had met his death at the hands of a gang of young thugs.

What remained of the castle stood on an outthrust point, with a dry moat around three sides of it. The fourth side dropped away five or six hundred feet to where the pewter curve of the river gleamed. There was a wooden bridge across the moat built on the broken arch of an earlier stone one, and I walked over to the shattered towers of the gatehouse and stood looking into the courtyard.

There really wasn't much left of the place. The shell of the original square keep, its gray stones full of holes like tattered chain mail, rose on one side with a few connecting fragments of wall and window where the great hall and the solar had been. Fallen blocks marked the line of most of the outer defenses, with some stretches ten or fifteen feet high rising here and there to show how strong they had once been. The only part that was relatively whole was a tower at one end of the outer corners and, built into one of its walls, a fine small chapel. It was here that most of the work was being done.

The workmen had put up a shed in the courtyard in which there were blocks of cut stone, stacks of timber, and large sheets of glass standing on end and reflecting the gatehouse. A man in thick corduroys and a flannel shirt was mixing cement in a wheelbarrow. I went over to talk to him. It wasn't until I got to the shed that I saw that the tower and chapel were islanded from the rest of the castle by a narrow but deep cleft.

I remembered the guide book. Somewhere under a guard tower, in some lower vault, the gunpowder had been kept and had blown up. It had taken with it part of the outer wall that overlooked the valley. There must have been a fault in the rock and this had gone as well, leaving a gaping crack that ran all the way back to the opposite wall, the one nearest the gatehouse. The ancient paving of cobbles had collapsed and now you could look down as through a slice out of a cake and see broken stone sixty feet or more below. Most of the length of it was fenced off, but a plank bridge spanned it just beyond the shed.

The workman smiled at me as I leaned over the wire fence to stare. You could look out at the valley through the outer end of the crack and it was a dizzying sight.

"A long way down, sir," he said. "Don't you get too near en. Us wouldn't want to climb down and pick up the pieces."

"Heights don't bother me," I said. "But what about you?"

He took hold of the handles of his wheelbarrow. "Nor me," he said.

He started across, the planks rattling under him. I followed him, to look at the chapel and tower from close by.

Another man who had been setting a stone in place, straightened up. "Hoy!" he called. "Don't come across there."

"I'm already across," I said.

"You shouldn't a done that, sir," the first man said, reproachfully. "There's no admittance to this part. Not till us've finished and fenced proper and built a proper bridge."

"It doesn't look to me as if that'll be until August or so," I said. "I don't expect to be here then. So as long as I'm here, why don't we forget it and you buy yourselves a couple of beers."

I put a fifty-pence piece into his knuckly hand. He said, "No need for that, sir," but slipped it into his pocket.

"You'd be American, by the way you talk, or Canadian," he said, picking up the wheelbarrow again and trundling it close to his partner.

"American." I peered in through the door of the chapel. "This must have been quite a place, once."

"You'll have nothing like it over in the States, I dare say," he said, smugly.

"Give us time," I answered.

Chapel and tower both had been roofed over and re-paired. The tower had a winding stair that led into upper chambers whose windows looked out over the panorama of the valley. The chapel's pointed windows were being fitted with clear panes of glass to provide enough light so that its fine tracery and carving would be seen; also, on one wall were some fragments of medieval painting which had somehow survived the centuries. New stonework was being fitted in here and there along the outer walls of both buildings.

The men went on with their work and let me prowl. After a time, I said, "I heard a man was murdered here not long ago."

"That's right," said the man in corduroys, straightening up. "Me and my mate come to work that morning and couldn't 'ardly get in for the policemen."

"How did it happen?"

"That I don't know. They'd taken en away by then, see, and wouldn't tell nothing to we. But the newspapers said them young yobs must a caught en here and stoned en to death."

I wasn't sure I'd understood him. "Stoned him to death?"

"Ar. Out there near the shed's where it happened. Us seen the bloodstains. And a right job us had sweeping up the glass. One of the stones hit some panes under the shed and smashed 'em to bits. And one hit Mr. Puncheon back o' the ear and done for 'im."

"That's a hell of a way to kill somebody," I said.

"Any way's a hell of a way, sir," said he. "If you wanted to know more about it, you'd ought to ask Colonel Hatch. He's the one found the poor gentleman."

"Colonel Hatch? Where's he?"

"Why, you can see his house from the gateway there, a little way along the common."

"Oh, well, it's got nothing to do with me, I guess," I said. "I was just curious."

"So was everybody," said the other man, fastidiously trimming away excess mortar with the point of his trowel. "You should a seen the crowds coming to look for a week afterward. And nothing for 'em to see. They'd done better to stay home and watch the telly. Take a bleedin' front seat for wars and riots and earthquakes whenever you like, so what they want to come 'ere for where there's nothing left to look at?"

"Ar, Perce," said the first man, spitting carefully at a snail. "But this 'ere, it was *real*, see?"

As I walked out between the crumbling towers of the gatehouse I thought about what the workman had said. It explained my own curiosity.

In a way, I knew George Puncheon. I could see the face in the photograph come alive. There was some humor in those pouchy eyes, and some complacency. I had thought of him as a man used to getting his way, stubborn and calculating, with enough taste to buy a good painting and enough vulgarity to buy those absurd statues. I could feel the currents of the community around him, respect mixed with detestation which had sounded in the tones of both Sterlet and Villiers; and surely even Mrs. Puncheon had betrayed some of the same dichotomy, telling me how much her husband had done for the community and yet joining forces against him? 'The man's death was, now that I had become even remotely involved with him, a more real occurrence than the shadowy violence one saw on television. I couldn't help wanting to know more about him. What on earth had drawn him to a place like the castle ruins at night? What could have provoked the skinheads to attack him?

So, almost without being aware of it, I found myself walking across the common towards the cottage the workmen had mentioned. It was not more than five hundred yards from the castle, on a little rise in the ground. It was small but trim, built I guessed in the 1920s, with a neat stone wall enclosing a lawn the size of a Ping Pong table but beautifully green and with a holly tree on each side of the door. On the gate, in neat metal letters, was the name: *The* (what else?) *Hollies.*

I paused with my hand on the gate and asked myself what I thought I was doing. I planned to barge in on a stranger to ask him impertinent questions about one of his neighbors. "Boorish American oaf!" he would snarl, and slam the door in my face. No, somehow that didn't go with what I knew about the English. He'd be icily polite: "I cannot see what possible concern it can be of yours." When they did that kind of thing it was worse than slamming doors.

I hung there debating and suddenly the front door opened and a thin, erect, gray-haired man in a tweed jacket came marching out. He had a big beak of a nose, beneath which was a neatly-clipped gray moustache. Neat—that was the word for everything about him, and he couldn't be anybody but the owner of the house.

He said, "I saw you hesitating and thought you might be lost. Can I help you?"

I said, "I was trying to make up my mind to do something which may offend you. I'll bet you're Colonel Hatch, aren't you?"

"I am. I don't understand. Why should you offend me? We don't know each other, do we?"

"No. The fact is, I wanted to ask you something but I wouldn't blame you if you told me it wasn't any of my business."

He said, with a smile, "It sounds very mysterious. Won't you come in?"

His sitting room was the kind of comfortable place you don't see any reason for ever moving out of. A couple of leather armchairs faced the spectacular valley view and at night could be turned around to the fire. Whisky and sherry stood on a sideboard. There were low bookshelves on each side of the fireplace, several of those warm eighteenth-century watercolors in which it's always sunset, and a couple of trophies of arms, one made up of curved Oriental weapons and the other of English swords, a crossbow with an ivory mounted stock, and a pair of long-barreled flintlock pistols. Over the fireplace hung a pair of crossed polo mallets and a silver shield-shaped plaque inscribed with the good wishes of the Islamabad Wanderers.

He saw me looking at this and said something in a guttural language.

"Sorry," I said. "I don't understand."

At once, he became very contrite. "I do beg your pardon," he said. "I thought you might speak Urdu. I am most frightfully sorry."

"I don't even know where Urdu is," I said. "But it doesn't matter, don't worry about it."

"It's one of the common languages of India."

"I see. Well, I can't blame you. As a matter of fact, I am an Indian. But—"

He cocked his head. "From the south? Do you speak Tamil?"

"No, sorry again. I never heard of it. My family lived in Oklahoma which isn't exactly the south, but before that they lived in Georgia."

He looked bewildered. "I'm afraid I don't know where either of those places is. Georgia? Surely that is in Russia?"

"There are people who wish it was, I suppose. It's in the United States."

I could almost hear something go *click*. "A Red Indian," he said. "That's what you meant."

"That's what I meant."

"Do forgive my bad manners. I shouldn't have assumed —You are on holiday, I suppose?"

"Not exactly. I'm here mainly on business."

"How very interesting."

"And you were talking about India. Is that where you served?"

"Among other places. But do sit down, Mr—?"

"Eddison."

"Tell me how you intended to offend me."

I said, "I'm a dealer in antiques and art, in the United States. I bought a small painting at an auction in Altoncester and I've been trying to find out something about it—where it came from, who owned it, who painted it. I've learned that the man who used to own it was murdered over in the ruins of the castle."

"George Puncheon."

"Yes. I got to talking with a couple of workmen in the castle and they told me you found his body."

"That's quite true."

I paused, feeling awkward. "I wonder if you can tell me anything about him."

He brushed a fingertip thoughtfully along the edge of his moustache. "Certainly," he said. "I can't imagine why you thought the question would offend me."

"It might seem like prying. Okay, it *is* prying. I don't know how to justify it except to say that I feel a kind of connection with Puncheon. We're connected through the picture I own now. Does that make sense?"

"I think so." His eyes went to the watercolors on the walls. "I'm very fond of those. One of them is by Turner. I should like to think that whoever owns it after I'm dead would be—sympathetic."

"A Turner? Which one?"

"That tiny landscape with the sunlight falling over the hills. My grandfather bought it when he was young. I have always been very attached to it. The river you see is the Severn and the spot where it was painted is not very far from here."

"It must be worth a fortune now."

"Possibly. I don't think my grandfather could have paid much for it. He hadn't any money." His sharp blue eyes glittered. "The man you're curious about, George Puncheon, liked it too. He tried several times to get me to part with it."

"I don't blame you for not selling it. It's lovely."

83

"I'm glad to hear you say so. But I wouldn't have sold it to him in any case. I doubt he thought of it as a painting by Turner."

"I don't follow you."

"He translated everything into profit and loss. He spoke a form of neo-Urdu, you might say. I mentioned Urdu before—it was originally the language spoken to subject peoples by their Mohammedan conquerors. Men like Puncheon are our new conquerors, and their language is money."

As he spoke, his tone grew sharper and I could hear the military ring in it.

"Yes," I said, "I've been told that's why he did so much for the village. Because it was profitable."

Colonel Hatch rose from his chair in an explosive movement, then, as if he were throttling down anger, stood with his hands behind his back looking out the big bay window.

In the quiet voice in which he generally spoke, he said, "To be fair, he did a good deal for the village—by his own lights. The estate houses, for instance. There was a need for new housing. We've had people moving here who work in the plants in Altoncester and Gloucester. I don't suppose one can complain overmuch at Puncheon's having filled the need. The tradesmen are pleased. More people means more business for them. But have you seen the wretched hovels he built? Flimsy, ugly, cramped, they'd be a disgrace to a self-respecting army encampment. They've been up a trifle over a year and their plaster is cracking. The window frames no longer fit and some of the doors are warped.

"But that's all part of the vocabulary of neo-Urdu. It's deplorable but it isn't what I hate most. No—they don't look as though they belonged in Chaworth at all."

He jammed his hands into his jacket pockets as if he couldn't keep them still. "I take it you've seen the village? The houses were built with pride and care. Every house meant a family, people who had their roots here. And now for the first time in our history we can display a slum. What do you suppose that estate will look like in ten years, or twenty? What do you imagine will be left of the village?"

The emphasis had gone out of his tone to be replaced with melancholy. "I'm very sorry," he said. "I shouldn't have subjected you to that but when I begin riding my hobby-horse. . ."

"I know how you feel," I said. "I guess a lot of people must have been just as happy when Puncheon was killed."

"I'd have killed him myself if I had thought I could get away with it," Hatch said, crisply. "He was to have visited me the very evening he was murdered. Curious that we should have spoken of the Turner because he said he wanted to talk to me about it again, that he had another offer to make me. He phoned and said he'd be late. He never came. I thought it odd, but I couldn't have cared less. I supposed he had changed his mind.

"I was reading, here in this room, and heard a tremendous rattling and banging—the noise of an old car driving across the common. I looked out and saw the headlights over there at the castle. I had heard about those young hooligans kicking up a fuss at the Fleece the night before—everyone in the village knew about that—and I wondered if they could be up to some mischief. After a bit, I got my stick and went to see. I have a sentimental attachment to the castle."

I could imagine this tough old boy with his stick, confronting a gang of rowdies, and somehow the odds didn't seem too great.

He went on, "I hadn't gone a hundred yards before the car drove off again. I decided they hadn't been there long enough to do any serious damage and in any case, if they had, it was too late to stop them. So I came along home."

He shook his head. "If I had gone on to the moat I'd have

seen Puncheon's car parked there. It was a bright moon-light night. However, to be cold-blooded about it, it would have done him no good. He was dead by then. I walked over early next morning, and that's when I found him."

"The workmen told me he'd been stoned to death."

"Not exactly. The boys pelted him with steel balls. Ball-bearings, you know, an inch or two in diameter." He made a circle with thumb and forefinger to show me. "There's a plant in Altoncester that makes them, and the police inspector told me that some of the lads work there. I understand they have been known to put the balls in a stocking and use them as weapons. In this case, they seem to have thrown them, and one hit Puncheon behind the ear. The police questioned a number of the boys—skin-heads, I understand they call them now—but nothing could ever be made to stick and no proof was ever found that they'd done it."

"But why?" I asked. "What could have brought him to the castle at that hour? And what could he have done to make the boys start throwing steel balls at him?"

"I can't answer your first question. I don't think anyone will ever know. As for the second, Puncheon was what I can only describe as an eminently killable man. I shouldn't imagine it would take much, in any case, to bring out the devil in these lads. From the little I've seen of them, they strike me as a thoroughly wicked lot. I've seen a good deal of violence at one time or another," he added, his voice even gentler than it had been, "and nothing men do to each other surprises me."

I could guess that. He had obviously not been the kind of officer who sits counting forms somewhere in the rear.

"Were you in the army long?" I asked.

"All my life. I was a professional. So was my father, and his father as well."

"You couldn't have picked a nicer spot to retire to," I said.

He nodded. "As a matter of fact, I was born here. Oh, not in this house of course, I meant the village. There have always been some of us in Chaworth."

It was an echo of what Jill had said to me. I couldn't help a pang of jealousy. My family, my whole people come to that, could have said the same thing once about another place, but they had long been dispossessed. When you came right down to it I was as rootless in my own country as I was here.

I put that thought aside and got up. "I won't take any more of your time," I said. "Thanks very much. You've certainly answered my question."

"Must you go?" he said. "It's been a great pleasure to talk to you. Won't you have a glass of sherry? Or perhaps whisky would be more to your taste."

He sounded as if he genuinely wanted me to stay. "I can't turn down whisky," I said. "Just a small one."

"Excellent! I don't generally drink at this hour but I'll join you, as you're a guest who has come so far." He went to the decanter and poured out a couple of drinks. "I hope you like single malt. This is Laphroig."

"I've never had it."

"Then let me urge you not to put any water in it."

I sipped the stuff. It had a rich, heavy, smoky taste. "Great," I said.

"Twelve years old," he said, reverently. "You can taste the peat in it. It is lovely, isn't it?"

"I've never tasted anything like it. Do you mind if I have a closer look at that Turner, by the way?"

"By all means."

It was even lovelier than the whisky. Hatch beamed at my comments. Then I looked at the other pictures, and then at the weapons.

"Those were used by various members of the family," he explained.

They were a kind of military history of Britain.

On the mantelpiece stood a photograph in a silver frame, of a rather formidable-looking gray-haired woman with haughty eyes.

"My wife," Hatch said.

"I'd like to meet—" I began, and then bit it off. Something suddenly told me that this was the house of a solitary man.

He said, gently, "She's dead. A most unfortunate accident. She was killed by a lorry, when they were building the estate on the edge of the village."

"I'm sorry," I said. Looking for a quick change of subject, I motioned to the polo mallets and the silver plaque.

"Who were the Islamabad Wanderers?" I asked.

"Oh, some chaps I played polo with a long time ago," he replied. "Do you know the game?"

"I've never seen it."

"It's worth seeing." His face lighted up. "You must let me introduce you to it. There is polo every Sunday at Altoncester Park. Would you like to go?"

"Yes, I would, if I can manage it."

"Will you still be here on Sunday?"

I had promised Jill I'd wait three days, and Sunday would be the third day. "It's very possible."

"Where are you staying? The King's Head? Ah, Mrs. Orchard's done wonders with the place. Well, now, suppose I ring you Sunday morning and if you're free we can fix things up."

"That'll be fine."

I glanced at my watch. I didn't want to outstay my welcome. He insisted on walking with me back to the castle, where I'd left the car. He chose a stick out of a stand in the hall and we strode along together across the grass.

"How do you like being in England?" he said.

I began to say something glib and trivial, but glancing

sidelong at him I saw that he really seemed to want to know. It wasn't merely polite conversation.

"I'm split," I said. "It's not just liking or not liking this country. It goes deeper. I find myself drawn to the leisurely pace—or what seems leisurely to me, although it may not to you. I find myself repelled by a kind of bland stupidity—" I stopped and thought. "No, I'm not saying it quite right. I haven't seen all that much of your country and maybe I don't have the right to draw conclusions."

"Please go on."

"Let me tell you a story. I was riding on a London bus with an English dealer I know. He asked the conductor for two five-penny fares. I found out that the fare is different depending on how far you ride, so I said to him, 'How does the conductor know you're telling the truth? Maybe you ought to be paying twice as much.' 'Oh, no,' he said, 'I wouldn't do that, you know.' He wasn't unique. Everybody does it. Well, look—this is the only country I know where you say how much you want to pay for a bus ride and the conductor trusts you.

"Another thing. I remember hearing an announcement on television one night. The announcer said, 'The Wednesday play is being shown at a later hour than usual tonight because certain things in the second act are rather frightening and we want to be sure no small children are watching.' How about that? And even more to the point: I remember a news broadcast on TV once in which the newscaster said something like, 'The war scenes which follow are not for the squeamish.'

"That stuff—I call that civilized."

He laughed. I went on, "Sure, but this is also the country that rewards jockeys with knighthoods but ignores the poverty of its writers and artists. It's the country which can be depended on to rise in arms against cruelty to horses but doesn't seem to care much about cruelty to babies—at any rate there's no Royal Society for the Prevention of Cruelty to them. You're small and tight and you've had to learn how to get along together, but it's bred some funny provincial qualities, some short-sightedness along with the tolerance.

"You stick to a lot of inefficiency because it's the way things were always done. But then you let yourselves be seduced like a bunch of hillbillies by gimcrackery that looks modern and shiny although it's as shoddy as last year's chrome plate. You've improved the standard of cooking so that you can get good French or Italian or Chinese food all over England now, but you can't find any good English food. You cut down your hedgerows so that you can increase the profits from bigger fields, but you don't seem to see that you're destroying the very thing that has preserved the English topsoil for centuries.

"I could go on—but what the hell, maybe what it amounts to is that you've got the same faults everybody else has, but that everything looks bigger on this smaller landscape."

He swung his stick at a buttercup. "If you are criticizing us, I must say you're doing so in a most flattering way."

"All right," I said, "You tell me what *you* think about your country."

He was silent for a spell. We had come to the castle by then, and he stared up at the broken towers of the gatehouse.

Then he murmured, "Oh, I hardly think I have anything to say that would be of much interest."

His blue eyes were clear and candid but it was as if he had shut a window. I could still see him on the other side of it but the sound had been cut off.

I liked him, though, and I let him off the hook. "You're too modest," I said smiling. "But let it go. I'll hear from you on Sunday, then, right?"

"Yes, certainly."

I got into my car and as I drove off he raised his stick to me in salute, as if it were a sword. He looked right, somehow, standing in front of that castle.

90

A line from the guide book I had read floated into my memory. "The seneschal was Bogo de Hacche, a noted warrior, whose family held the castle until the 15th century."

The recognition gave me a physical jolt. No wonder he had a sentimental attachment to the place.

I drove around exploring the countryside for a few hours. Then I remembered that Sterlet was having dinner with me at seven and I turned back. I parked the car in the lot behind the hotel and got out, planning my time in my head. I could spend a couple of hours with him before I needed to start for Altoncester and my meeting with Thompson, the dealer.

A man had been leaning against the wall, so motionless, blending so well with it, that I never noticed him until he moved forward.

"Beg your pardon, sir," he said.

"I know you, don't I?" I said. "I met you in that pub with Sterlet. William. That right?"

He nodded. "I've come about Sir Donald, see," he said. He had that hunter's trick of pitching his voice to carry only to the person he was addressing.

"What about him?"

" 'e won't be coming to dinner."

"Oh? How come?"

" 'e's sloshed, sir."

I was reminded of the way Colonel Hatch had looked at me. William's gaze was as innocent and direct. But the same curtain was down. I recalled the scene in the pub. Sterlet had said something that had made both William and the publican uneasy. I was willing to bet there was something more than I was getting here. Perhaps William had seen to it that Sterlet would be too drunk to talk to me?

I said, "That's too bad. And what about my painting?"

"Painting, sir?"

"Didn't he say anything about it? If he told you he was meeting me for dinner—and I suppose he must have or you wouldn't be here—he must have said something about the painting I bought from him."

William shook his head. "I don't know about that."

I felt drawn to him. That stolid, expressionless face which gave nothing away made him like one of the Ani-Kituhwagi. He could have been a relative. *Gonyoliga'*, I said to him, in my head. *I'skuya gigagen.* But of course, he couldn't understand. To him, *I* was white.

I said, "Well, thanks for telling me. I hope he'll be all right."

"I dare say 'e'll live."

He was turning away when on impulse I said, "Do you hunt?"

To my surprise, the façade cracked into a grin. "Me?" he said. "I never been 'orseback in my life."

"Horseback? What's that got to do with it?" I said.

"Why, 'untin'."

"Oh. Fox hunting. No, I meant going out with a gun after game."

The grin was still there, but smaller and more private now. "Us dursn't, sir," he said. "They'd 'ave the law a'ter we."

"Sure, I understand. That's why it's smart to take walks on nice quiet moonlight nights. I've done it myself," I said.

He was grave again. I could see him considering me and all my works and suddenly I wished I had kept my big mouth shut.

But all he said was, "Ar. Well, goodnight, sir."

He went off across the market square. But I was now pretty sure I knew what Sterlet had meant when he had said that William had his reasons for walking near the castle at night. Rabbits, I supposed, or whatever small game they had around here. I wondered whether he'd had

93

any other reason on that particular night. I made a mental note to ask somebody what William thought about Puncheon. Then I crossed it out. It was all very puzzling, but it really wasn't my affair. The last thing I wanted to do was get involved with some kind of country feud, which was what this looked more and more like being.

Dinner was plain and hearty, a pleasant contrast to the complaint I'd made to Hatch, and I ate my words with pleasure, along with a solid mixed grill with vegetables from local gardens and a pint of the local bitter, a nice snappy beer. The dining room was quiet and comfortable and looked out towards a side street which ended in a huge sky streaked with banners of cloud, gold-edged, dark gray and purple.

I killed time until nine and then started for Altoncester. The sky was still light, the fringes of the clouds still shot with sunset, for at this time of year in England it doesn't get absolutely dark until after ten. But as I dropped down the long hill into the valley the twilight thickened about me like mist. There were lights in Altoncester, the traffic had vanished and the streets were empty. I got a little lost, owing to the fact that street names were hard to find, but eventually I made it to the south side of the town and parked in a main road off which, according to the map Mrs. Orchard had given me, Brewers Lane led.

It was a neighborhood of dingy two-story houses, overshadowed by the steel drum of a gas works. It smelled of cabbage and coal smoke with an undercurrent of gas. Through lacy curtains I could see the pallid flickering of television screens. The harsh glare of street lamps emphasized the dirty brick of the housefronts and picked out crumpled newspaper, empty milk bottles, cartons of rubbish bursting their seams.

I walked along Brewers Lane and saw the pub sign on a corner, a gold trumpet darkened by soot. There were half a dozen figures standing under a street lamp nearby and as I crossed they turned to look at me.

They were young, the oldest of them about nineteen. They all wore their hair short, almost down to the scalp, which gave them the look of Prussian conscripts. They wore jackets and ties, most of them, and had a tidy appearance but their air of respectability was spoiled by thick clumpy shoes, like army boots.

They were between me and the pub and I started to pass them. They spread out, deliberately blocking the way, and I had to stop.

One of them, the tallest, who had a round, fattish, pimply face, said, "What's your hurry, Packey?"

I eyed them. I didn't like this situation at all. They stood grinning, and that and the fact of their youth made it all seem harmless enough, just horsing around. But I didn't like it. It woke an echo in my memory, a bunch of kids on Wyatt Street stopping me on my way to school with just such cheerful grins and saying, "Hey, Nig, you new around here?" before they ganged up on me.

I said, carefully, "You've got the wrong man. My name isn't Packey."

I started to go around them, choosing the end where there was a runty one whose rosy cheeks made him look about twelve years old.

They closed up in front of me. The leader said, "Cor! Ain't we dainty? 'My name isn't Packey.' " He said it mincingly, and the others giggled in appreciation.

He stepped nearer. "We got no time for wogs around here, see?"

I backed away a little. All I could think of was the painting under my arm. If they started something, the brown paper wrapping wouldn't be enough to protect it. I shifted it, to get it behind me.

The movement caught their attention, and one of them said, "He's got something, Des."

"Ooh, a box of choclits," said another.

95

I could feel the sweat start under my arms and roll cold down my ribs. I said, as pacifically as I could, "Look, I don't want any trouble—"

"There won't be no trouble," said the leader. "Just you let us 'ave a look at what's in the parcel, Packey."

At this point I decided that Mr. Thompson could go on sitting in the pub all night. I didn't want to risk having a hole through the middle of the painting and I didn't want a fight, certainly not six against one.

I was about to turn and walk away as quickly as I could, when the leader made a grab for the picture. He almost got it. I twisted aside. One of the others kicked at me.

The heavy boot caught me, fortunately not on the edge of the shin, but on the side of it. I went staggering against the frame of a house door and almost fell over the doorstep. Milk bottles clinked and rattled underfoot. The pain dazzled up from my leg and exploded in my head so that for a moment I couldn't see. But I could hear all right. The kids were laughing.

The laughter snapped me into a cold rage. The boys were moving in on me. I snatched up one of the empty milk bottles and gave it a rap against the edge of the stone stoop. The bottom cracked off just the way I wanted it. I straightened with my eyes fixed on the leader of the gang.

"Okay, you son of a bitch," I said. "Come on."

He didn't believe I'd do it. He kicked at me but I was ready now. I moved sideways and in on him while he was unbalanced, and stabbed at him with the jagged glass. I was so far gone in my fury that I almost let him have it in the face, but at the last minute I was able to change my mind and I hit him in the shoulder instead. I weigh 180 pounds and a lot of it was behind the blow.

He went down like a sack and I could hear the smack of his head against the sidewalk. I whirled on the others, marking the next one I'd take. I could feel my lips pulling against my teeth, and the bloody glass glittered in my hand. I must have looked like a bad dream. They turned and ran.

96

It wasn't only me that had made them run, though. There were people coming out of the pub. I stood and slowly let the anger go out of me. My ears were ringing and I heard myself say, "Somebody better call the cops."

I dropped the broken bottle. I suddenly remembered the painting, and found that I was holding it so tightly against my body that my arm hurt. The kid on the ground was still out and there was blood spreading slowly under him, black in the lamplight.

Somebody said to me, "Are you hurt?"

"I'm all right," I said. "You'd better look at that guy."

"You was as good as him," somebody else said. "You should 'a done the lot."

A big police car had drawn up, and a couple of cops were out of it as soon as it stopped. One of them said, "What's happened here, then?" The other knelt next to the kid. "We'll want the ambulance," he said, and went back to the car to phone.

I said, "That one on the ground—he was one of a gang that jumped me. I hit him with that broken milk bottle, and the rest ran."

The policeman looked me over carefully. "Did anyone else see it happen?" he asked.

One of the men said, "It's just like what he says. I seen it, all right, the end of it anyhow. We've had trouble with these here skinheads before. It's getting so the streets ain't hardly safe."

The policeman asked a few more questions and wrote down a couple of names and addresses. The ambulance, its blue light flashing, came down the street and the kid was lifted into it.

"I shall have to ask you to come along to the station, sir," the policeman said to me. "We'll have to have the whole story, you understand."

At the police station, I was shown into a dung-colored room furnished with a couple of straight chairs, a table, and a poster urging people to lock their cars. A sad, thin, tired-looking man in a shiny blue suit came in, motioned

97

me to a chair, and sat down on the edge of the table.

In a cold, precise voice, he said, "Will you state your name, please?"

A uniformed cop had taken the other chair and opened a shorthand pad.

"Robert Eddison," I said. I gave him one of my business cards.

"Connecticut?" He raised an eyebrow. "American, eh? May I see your passport?"

I handed it over. There was a note in his voice I didn't much care for.

I said, "Aren't you going to try to round up the rest of those kids?"

His glance was hard. "We'll take everything in due course, if you don't mind. Suppose you tell me what happened."

I went over the story again. When I had finished, he said, "I see. How did you come to be in that neighborhood?"

I stared at him. Remembering what Villiers had said about Thompson, I didn't intend to answer that question.

I said, "I don't see what that has to do with it. Surely, I have a right to be in any neighborhood I want to?"

He got off the table. "You don't seem to realize," he said, "that this sort of violence is a serious offence. Stabbing somebody—"

I broke in on him. "You don't seem to realize that I was the one who was attacked by half a dozen thugs on a public street. I suppose if they had left me smashed to a pulp you'd have arrested me for blocking traffic, is that it? What the hell do you think you're up to? Don't you think a man has the right to defend himself when people try to beat him up? You're a little mixed up about who committed the crime."

He didn't say anything for a moment or two. Then he took out a pack of undersized, cheap cigarettes and offered me one.

"All right," he said. "Don't get worked up."

I sat back. "Okay. Thanks, but I don't smoke."

"Very wise." He lit one, and then went on, "Now, let me make something clear to you. However it looks to you—and I don't say you mightn't have had some right on your side—the fact is that there was a fight in the street and you stabbed a man with a broken bottle. If he should be prepared to bring a charge of assault against you, I'd have no option but to arrest you and bring you into court. I wouldn't like that and neither would you. Right? We've had a good deal of difficulty with these skinheads lately, suspicions of very serious crimes—"

"Murder, for instance."

"You've heard about it, have you? Very well, then you can see that I don't want any trouble like this in my parish, and I certainly don't want the kind of situation where an American visitor is going to be up against a charge of assaulting one of *them*."

I was partly mollified. "Okay, but you do see my side of it?"

"I see it. Suppose you tell me what you were doing in an unsavory neighborhood like Brewers Lane."

I had already figured out what to say. "I was just driving around sight-seeing. It didn't look like such an unsavory neighborhood to me. You haven't seen unsavory neighborhoods in America, or you wouldn't be surprised. I thought it would be interesting to go into a pub for a drink. I had the painting in my car and I didn't want to leave it behind. That's all."

He grunted. "I wish tourists would stay where they belonged."

There was a rap at the door. He went over and talked in a soft voice with someone. Then he came back and dismissed the stenographer.

"Well, Mr. Eddison," he said, "you've had a narrow squeak. I've just had a phone call from the police officer in

99

the hospital. That young chap wasn't badly hurt, just a lump on the head and a couple of stitches in the shoulder. He says he was running along and fell over and cut himself on a broken milk bottle."

I must have looked my astonishment, because he suddenly smiled in a very human manner. "They don't like the police much, those lads. He'd stand up in court against one of *us,* all right, if we pushed him around a bit, but he won't give us any satisfaction against someone else."

"That's the end of it then, I suppose?"

"You're well out of it."

"I've got a bruise the size of an egg on the side of my shin."

"You can be grateful it was nothing worse."

It seemed to me he was being very smug about it. Everything was safely back where it had been and there wouldn't be any discomfort for the cops. Somebody might have asked him disagreeable questions, like, how come you allow gangs like this to roam around knocking over the citizenry?

"I'll have a constable drive you back to your car," he said. "After this, I suggest you confine your sight-seeing to the beaten path."

I restrained myself from thanking him for his advice. In the waiting room outside, a man who had been lounging against the information desk stopped me.

"Excuse me," he said. "I'm Daley, *Gloucestershire Star.* Can I have a word with you?"

"I was just going to be driven back to my car."

"I'll be glad to drive you back." He nodded to the policeman with me. "You won't mind, Albert. It'll give you time for another cuppa."

"What do you want to talk to me about?" I asked, as he walked to his car, a much-dented old Morris.

"I hear you were in a dust-up with a gang of skinheads. And you hurt one of them and drove the rest off. Would you mind giving me the story?"

"There isn't all that much to tell."

We sat in his car and he made notes while I wearily told the story for the third time.

"That's grand!" he said. "It takes one of you Yanks to come over and show us how to handle these yobbos."

"Listen, do me a favor and don't play that up," I said. "I'm a quiet, hard-working dealer, not the Daredevil Swordsman of Old New England. And in any case, I don't think you can use any of this because the kid I stabbed says he was just running quietly along minding his own business and tripped and cut himself."

"He said that? Damn it, then there's no case. Hmm. I'll have to make a few changes, leave out the broken bottle. But never mind," he said, brightening, "there's still plenty of human interest in it. For instance, I'd like to know what you think of England—how you like it over here, you know, and how long you've been here and so on."

I told him briefly, for I was beginning to feel tired. When he'd had enough, he thanked me and drove me to the street where I'd left my car.

"There was one funny thing about that attack tonight," I said, on the way. "Maybe you can tell me. Have you ever heard of someone named Packey?"

He shook his head. "Why?"

"They kept calling me that. They obviously mistook me for somebody else."

He glanced sidelong at me. "Oh," he said. "*They* called you. . .No, what they were calling you was short for Pakistani. Paki. That's what they took you for. It's their chief sport, what they call Paki-bashing."

"I see," I said, sourly. "I was an un-English color, eh?"

"I'm sorry. We're not all like that, you know."

I began to laugh. "Christ! That's the second time in one day that I've been the wrong Indian."

"The second time?"

"Oh, this morning was much pleasanter." I told him about Colonel Hatch.

He pulled up behind my car and stopped. He turned in his seat to stare at me. "Then you're a Red Indian? A real one?"

"Don't start that, for Christ's sake," I said. "Everybody I mention it to expects me to whip out a tomahawk. I was brought up in Connecticut and I still live there, and I don't go hunting buffalo unless they're painted ones or nineteenth-century bronzes."

"But still. . ." he said, wistfully.

"I know. You all once read *The Last of the Mohicans* and went to see John Ford Westerns. So did I. It was just as romantic for me when I was a kid, and just as unreal. No, let's drop it."

"If you say so."

"I've got another question for you. Do you remember the murder of a man named George Puncheon?"

"Yes. A few months ago, in Chaworth. Why?"

"This painting I've got here used to belong to him and I've been curious about him. I wonder whether you know anything about what he was doing at the castle or why he was killed?"

"Only what was in the papers. I take it you know all that."

"Yes. And after tangling with these kids I can understand how he might have said something that started them off. They're vicious little pricks, aren't they? And I was just talking this morning about how civilized England is. You've got the same fester under the skin everybody else has."

"Oh, true. But we're not quite so far gone as some countries."

"Yes, you don't give live ammunition to amateur soldiers, or try to drown out your violence with even more virtuoso performances of official violence. Anyway, to come back to Puncheon, did you ever meet him?"

"Several times. He was often at the head of committees,

102

or delivering speeches, that sort of thing. Then there was the business of that woman's death."

"What was that?"

"When he was building the estate houses on the edge of Chaworth. A woman was hit and killed by one of the lorries. A lot of people said it was Puncheon's fault because, you see, although there was a back road the lorries could have taken he had insisted that they drive through the village as being the shortest route. There was a good deal of ill feeling over the affair. And soon after there was the furore over his roadstone quarry."

"I heard about that, too. And I couldn't help being curious about his wife joining the—what was it?—Committee for the Preservation of Old England?"

"Council for the Protection of Rural England. They're a sort of watchdog organization, people all over the country keeping an eye on things like new planning, pollution, industries and that sort of thing. There's quite an active branch in Altoncester, and one in Chaworth which Mrs. Puncheon helped form."

"His wife started the opposition?"

"I shouldn't have put it quite that way. This was before the matter of the quarry came up. Then, last autumn, Puncheon made his application for permission to knock down an old house called Pellet Lane and begin quarrying stone. At that point the CPRE got up in arms. They had some members on the County Council and carried the vote to refuse his application. He then appealed to the Ministry and a public inquiry was to be held.

"There was some talk about whether Mrs. Puncheon would resign from the CPRE. She didn't. On the other hand, she never publicly opposed her husband. But she had helped organize the branch, and she remained an officer of it. Most people took it to mean that, however quietly, she was against his project."

"It figures. What happened at the public inquiry?"

103

"It never came off. Puncheon's death put an end to the whole business. He had bought up Pellet Lane years before as an investment. He probably knew that the roadstone was under it. He let the house fall to bits to save the trouble of knocking it down until he was ready. Now, of course, it's safe in his wife's hands. She owns all the property."

I said, "I wonder how she came to oppose him over the matter? When I talked to her, she kept telling me what a fine man her husband had been."

"Loyal to the core, eh? Yes, but she's County, you see. He wasn't."

"I don't know what that means."

He drummed his fingers on the steering wheel. "No, you haven't anything like that in the States, I suppose. Well, let's see. Puncheon had come up the hard way. You could still hear it in his speech. Bristol working-class family, but he'd managed to shed most of his background. Solid Tory, always good for opening a bazaar, played golf but didn't ride, drove a Daimler, nothing ostentatious or radical about him, what his friends called a sound chap. But all the same, he was an outsider. Whereas his wife—she came from here, she was a Huntercombe, related to the Sterlets. Chaworth Court, that house she lives in, that was hers, not his. Her sense of responsibility to the village was different from his. That's why they naturally stood on opposite sides. Do you see?"

"Frankly," I said, "no. What do you mean, 'Her sense of responsibility was different from his'?"

"Put it this way. Everything he did he probably did from a feeling that the village could only be bettered if you made it move with the times, built houses, brought industry there, made it more up-to-date. While for her, it would be a matter of protecting it from corrosive changes, keeping our heritage against the un-English tide."

It sounded like a jeer, and yet there was a serious undertone in his voice.

"What about you?" I asked.

104

"Me? I don't think she and her lot have a chance," he said, briskly. "In another ten years—or if not that, in twenty—villages like Chaworth will have been swallowed up. They're already anachronisms. You can't stop it."

"And you think that's good?"

"What's the difference what I think? It's inevitable," he said, with a finality that ended the discussion.

I slept until nine-thirty, which I seldom do, and had breakfast sent up to my room which I never do. But this morning I felt I needed solitude and pampering. Pampering, because I ached and my shin hurt like hell and I had a bruise on my left biceps where I had hit the edge of the door after the kid had kicked me. I hadn't even noticed it the night before but it was painful this morning. Solitude, because I was in a peculiar state of mind.

I kept thinking how mad the world was. A pack of hoods had jumped me because they thought I was one kind of Indian. But almost everyone I had met received me with naive delight because I was another kind of Indian. That led me to think about England in a way I hadn't really done before. The violence of last night brought things into a bizarre focus. I found I was angry that they should do *that* sort of thing in *this* place.

Now, why? I had no stake in this country. I didn't even like it all that much. But the things I'd said to Colonel Hatch off the top of my head came back to me. When you had come to meet the English you found that they really accepted what others only seem to give lip service to: the idea of each man as an individual. With us, people tend to become political abstractions, objects or properties. More than that, the English cared about their land in a way that appealed to me, for my people had had their land deep in their guts and had lost it. Without doubt, the English must have their share of superficial patriots and flag-wavers but I hadn't met much of that. I had met instead a profound attachment to place, to history, to the values of continuity and community which seemed to me to give them a thread of strength, unobtrusive but enough to hold them all. And so infractions were magnified here; an antisocial act stood out more shockingly because it was a personal affront. Such an act was, just as the workman at the castle had said, something *real.* And it seemed to me that we, in America, were in danger of forgetting that. It was we who had come to think in terms of "body counts" and "over-kill" or, on the other hand, "revolutionary confronta-tions." Our nice vocabulary of generalizations had blinded us to the real things done to real individuals.

But then I withdrew from making comparisons. I didn't know enough to do so, and maybe there isn't any way of comparing one country with another that makes any sense. Only, dimly, I now felt I understood a little more about these people. And I understood, too, a little more about what went on in Jill. I had known with my intelligence the factors that made decision hard for her. Now I had moved closer to knowing it deeper down, in my imagination.

I sat musing for a long time, looking out the window at the quiet market square. I was jolted by the buzz of the room phone.

A familiar, loud, hearty voice said, "Villiers here. Is that Mr. Eddison?"

"Yes, that's right."

"I understand you had quite an adventure last night."

"Yeah? How'd you come to hear about it?"

"Thompson rang me up this morning. He said he was nearly frightened out of his wits."

"Really? Too bad. I was kicked to pieces by a mob of skinheads and he was frightened."

"Come, come, Mr. Eddison. Surely you can understand

his position, the police turning up and so on?"

"Sure, I understand it."

"You can hardly blame him for what happened."

"Okay. I don't blame him. Now what? When can I get together with him?"

"Naturally, after what happened, he is more reluctant than ever to meet you anywhere publicly."

"I see. That makes things complicated, doesn't it?"

"I had a long talk with him, and I think I see a way out of the situation. Why don't you come along to my place at about four, for tea?"

"And then?"

"Then perhaps I'll have something for you."

"All right," I said. "I'll be there. But look Mr. Villiers, it had better be something conclusive."

"I'm certain we can settle the matter," he said. "Four o'clock, then? Right you are."

He hung up. I glanced at my watch and saw that it was nearly noon. I had pissed away the whole morning. "So what?" I told myself. "I'm just marking time waiting for Jill to make up her mind. There's no sweat. I'm not going anywhere."

I shaved and finished dressing. I got out the painting and inspected it to make sure it hadn't been damaged in the scuffle, but it was in good shape. I couldn't help admiring it again. I wondered what Maxwell's own work was like, because he was one hell of a good copyist.

That reminded me that I had a piece of unfinished business to attend to, Sterlet's picture. I still wanted it. I decided that I'd go over and see him after lunch, pay him, and pick up his painting.

I went downstairs. Lunch wasn't until one, and I sat in the lounge, had a beer, and picked up the local paper, the *Star*. And there I was on the front page: *Red Indian on Warpath Scalps Skinheads*.

I began reading, between annoyance and amusement.

A gang of toughs got more than they bargained for last night when they chose to attack an American visitor, Mr. Robert Eddison, of Connecticut. Mr. Eddison, an antique dealer on a visit to England, was exploring some of the quainter back streets of Altoncester when he was assaulted by. . .

I was interrupted by the moon-faced young man who served as Mrs. Orchard's maitre d'hôtel, if that isn't too lush a term for a combined porter, odd job man, and head waiter.

"Telephone for you, Mr. Eddison."

I took it in the booth up on the first floor landing. It was Mrs. Puncheon.

"I have just seen the paper," she said, "and I felt I must tell you how shocked and outraged I am. Are you—you weren't badly hurt, I hope?"

"Luckily, no, just a few bruises."

"Mr. Eddison, I hope you won't judge us all by that dreadful incident," she said, earnestly. "It is most unfortunate that you should have had such a bad introduction to Gloucestershire."

"It wasn't exactly an introduction—"

"I am having one or two people for dinner tonight. I wondered whether you could possibly manage to come. I should so much like you to meet some of my friends. Perhaps it would help give you a different impression."

"That's very kind of you, Mrs. Puncheon," I said, when I could get the words out. "I mean it. There's no need—but yes, I'd be delighted to come."

"That's splendid. Now, I must ask you one other question and I hope you'll forgive me if it sounds impertinent. I don't know what the custom is in your country—Do you dress for dinner?"

It took me a minute to get it. "Sometimes," I said. "But I'm sorry to say I haven't a dinner jacket with me."

"Ah, yes, of course. I see," she said. "Well, then, we'll be quite informal. At seven-thirty. Will that suit you?"

I went to lunch still shaking my head. I was overcome. Imagine, I said to myself, that nice old horse thinking about the stranger in her midst. And more than that, making sure I wouldn't turn up in the wrong clothes. I remembered what that reporter had said about her. That, clearly, was part of the lady of the manor bit. What she had just done fell under the heading of bringing goodies to a sick tenant. I could joke about it, but at the same time I was deeply touched.

I had just pushed my coffee cup away when another phone call came. This time it was Colonel Hatch.

"I'm sorry to disturb you, but I couldn't help wondering—it was you, wasn't it, in the paper today?"

"You mean the fracas last night? It wasn't serious."

"I'm glad to hear you say so. I felt outraged, thoroughly outraged. It's disgraceful! And particularly infuriating since it seems the police aren't doing anything about it, at least according to the report I read."

"There wasn't anything they could do, Colonel."

"It's most kind of you to defend them. And you weren't hurt, I gather."

"Not at all. It's very kind of you to phone."

"The least I could do. Now, what about tomorrow? Do you feel up to coming with me to Altoncester Park?"

"The polo match, you mean? Yes, as far as I know there's no reason why I shouldn't. The only thing is—I may be seeing a young lady."

"I quite understand. Of course, if she'd like to come she'll be more than welcome. Let me leave my number with you. If I don't hear from you to the contrary, I'll pick you up at about two-thirty."

I hung up, thinking it was almost worth it to have been attacked.

And even Mrs. Orchard joined the club. As I was leaving the hotel, she appeared before me sturdily erect, fixing me with her company commander's eye.

"Albert has just shown me the report in the newspaper," she barked. "It's shameful! You should have told me last

110

night, Mr. Eddison. I have a cousin who is Chief Super-intendent of the CID in Bristol. I shall have a word with him—"

"No, no, Mrs. Orchard, don't do that," I said. "It's all right. The police did everything they could. There was no damage done, and the best thing is just to forget it."

"Hmph! I can't think what's happening to us all, these days. My father would have had that gang rounded up and clapped into gaol before you could say knife. You might have been seriously injured."

"Luckily I wasn't."

"Good. At least it appears you gave them a thorough trouncing."

And off she marched leaving me with the feeling that I had only just escaped a court-martial.

I walked across the village and up to the gates of Pellet Lane. I went through the courtyard and climbed the rickety steps.

The door was opened to my knock by a naked girl.

I do not generally let my face show much, an old tribal trick I've cultivated, and I don't think my eyebrows lifted perceptibly. I looked her up and down. She had a beer belly and heavy breasts and a sullen expression.

"Good morning," I said. "This *is* a pleasant surprise."

She pushed her hair away from her face without seeming to understand me. Behind her, I heard Sterlet laugh raucously.

He shoved her aside and grinned at me. "I thought you were my cousin Julia," he said. "That's why I made Gwen open the door. I hoped the shock would make Julia fall downstairs and break her neck."

"You don't sound as though you have a happy family life."

"She's rich," he said. "Who knows, she might leave me something."

He stepped back from the door. He was wearing nothing but a pair of jeans.

"Come in, dear boy," he said. "Do excuse the state of

111

the flat. We're all at sixes and sevens this morning."

The place stank. The chair was covered with the girl's clothes, so I stood. I didn't plan to stay long anyway.

"Are you shocked?" he said, peering at me.

"Do you want me to be?"

He blinked. "I hadn't thought about it from that angle," he said. "But I imagine you Americans are unshockable. We're an effete race, we English. Played out."

The girl had crawled into bed and pulled the covers over herself. She lit a cigarette. Sterlet fished around on the floor and found a bottle of cider. He unscrewed the top, took a drink, and passed the bottle over to her.

"Played out," he repeated, sadly. "If I had any guts I'd murder Julia the way her husband was murdered. But she'd probably leave all her money to the CPRE and other such worthy causes."

"That's right, I'd forgotten. Mrs. Puncheon's your cousin, isn't she?"

"You are perceptive. Have a drink? Gwen, stop hogging the bottle."

"No, thanks," I said. "I'm sorry you never got to have dinner with me. What happened? Did your buddy, William, get you plastered?"

"Nobody gets me plastered, dear boy. I'm perfectly capable of doing it all on my own."

"Well, I've come to pay you and pick up my picture."

"My picture, you mean. A nice point, that. It'll always be mine even though it's yours." He stumbled over to the stack of paintings and began leafing through them. "A bloody fine point. Can anyone ever own a work of art? It's a living thing. We don't approve of slavery any longer, do we?"

He straightened, dangling the small painting carelessly by a finger under the stretcher.

"Speaking of owning things, what about that nice little van Goyen of yours? Have you found out anything more about it?"

"Not much," I replied. "Have you ever heard of a dealer named Thompson? A fellow in Altoncester."

He seemed to hesitate, and then said, "No. I don't think so. Why?"

"I'm told he's the man who sold the landscape to Puncheon. I've been trying to meet him, but without much luck so far. And by the way," I added, casually, "how did you come to know it was by van Goyen?"

He squinted at me. "What do you mean? You told me when you showed it to me the other day."

"Not me."

"Well, whatever it says on the back—"

"What about Maxwell?"

"All right. Maxwell, then. Any name you like."

I began to be annoyed. I said, "It's a funny thing, Sterlet, but ever since we first met I've had the damndest feeling that you're skirting all around something, hinting, almost telling me, and then ducking away again. The landscape painting, Puncheon's death, that stuff you told me in the pub about walking at night. . .When you first saw my picture you said you'd seen it before. Then you denied it. Now you've just told me it's by van Goyen and then you pretend you never said it."

He stood quite still. His face, what I could see of it through the tangle of blond hair and beard, grew red.

"Are you quite finished?" he said.

"Let's say I am. What about it?"

"Do you mind telling me what right you think you have to cross-examine me?"

"No right at all. I came here in a friendly way and asked you a friendly question. I liked your work and we seemed to get along. But I don't like being made a fool of with barefaced lies."

"Are you calling me a liar?"

"Have you got a better word?"

"Don't you call *me* a liar."

"Do you really expect me to believe—"

113

"I don't care what you believe. You haven't any right to treat people as liars. Not when you come snooping around, asking all sorts of questions—"

"If you don't want to tell me anything, then tell me to mind my own business," I said, and by now I was in a real rage. "I'll take that. But don't keep handing me bullshit, saying first one thing and then another."

"If I do, you asked for it. Nothing that happens here is any of your affair. Least of all Puncheon's death. Or anything to do with him. You come here—"

"Okay. That's clear enough."

"—trying to find out I don't know what. William was right. Friendly questions, indeed. And being an American is bloody good cover, I suppose."

I didn't wait to hear any more. I made for the door before I could lose my temper completely and clout him.

He yelled after me, "You forgot your bloody painting. *My* work! The one you liked so much, you bastard!"

His little picture came flying past my head. It hit the wall with a flat slap and bounced to the floor.

I stepped over it and went out, slamming the door so that the building rattled. I ran down the stairs, heedless of the way they quaked under me. I strode off, taking the road away from the village, not caring where I went, just trying to walk off my anger.

It didn't take too long. The road I was on dipped downhill between high banks. Oaks and beeches shaded it, their roots snaking out to hang over my head. Sweet bird songs sounded from them. I was in a shady tunnel, which opened on my left from time to time to a view over the slopes to the river valley below. I stopped after a bit, leaned on a wooden gate mopping my face, and looked.

And I began to think more clearly about Sterlet's outburst. He had said some interesting things, only I couldn't remember them all. But my impression was that *he* thought *I* was the liar.

"William was right," he had said. About what? It could

only be about my being a stranger who had been asking prying questions that would threaten somebody. And that somebody must be Sterlet himself. I recalled how both William and the publican of The Fleece had closed in on him and how strong my impression had been that they'd tried to shut him up when he was talking about Puncheon's death. To protect him, what else?

A little thrill, a minor electric shock, ran through me. Suppose Sterlet had killed George Puncheon?

Take it easy, Ahuludegi, I said to myself. That is somewhat crazy.

But was it? Sterlet had little enough, and if Puncheon had gone through with the sale of the property he'd have had nothing, not even his miserable loft to live in. Whatever was left of his old home would have vanished into a quarry.

I had ample evidence that Sterlet didn't like Puncheon. And I had just had evidence that he had a temper.

There was something else, too, something that had been buried and which now came bobbing up in my memory like driftwood. When I had first visited Sterlet, he had stumbled and almost fallen because he had stepped on a round steel ball lying among the rubbish on the floor. Was it, I wondered, just such a steel ball as had hit Puncheon behind the ear?

I chewed that over for a minute and then I thought, But Colonel Hatch heard the skinheads drive up to the castle that night.

Aha! I thought, but he didn't see or hear Puncheon arrive. He had said to me, "If I'd walked up to the moat I would have seen Puncheon's car parked there." But he didn't walk up to the moat, and maybe Puncheon had come after the skinheads had been and gone. It was likely the police must have thought of that, and clearly they had nothing solid to go on, no way of proving that the kids had actually done it.

And what had Sterlet said in The Fleece? "Somebody

heard them drive up that night, but William was there and he never heard a thing." And he had also said, "I walk there sometimes and so does William, but we have our own reasons." I knew what William's reasons might be, but what about Sterlet's?

Suppose, I thought, William had seen Sterlet kill Puncheon? He never would have turned in a man whose family was so deeply tied up with the village. The way in which both the publican and William had treated him—"Now, Sir Donald," and with a look begging me to make him eat something—showed there must be some attachment there which I could understand although I'd never run across it before. They'd want to keep things quiet, keep suspicion away from their buddy the baronet. When I had come poking around, asking questions and buying drinks that loosened Sterlet up and made him talk indiscreetly, William's suspicions must have awakened. Maybe he thought I was a cop masquerading as an American. Of course! Hadn't Sterlet said that being an American was good cover?

That would explain a lot of things about the way Sterlet talked to me. And it would explain his last furious act, throwing the picture at me. No wonder! He had thought I liked his work and really wanted to buy it, and suddenly, if William had made his point, he had felt I was just trying a cheap trick to win his confidence. Nor could I attach any importance to anything he said about the Maxwell landscape. As far as he was concerned that might just be a way I'd use to get to him. I had made too much of the van Goyen business; after all, the label did say that it was copied from a van der Heyden and I couldn't expect him to remember clearly.

I wanted to go right back and have it out with him. But how could I? What could I possibly say or do that would convince him? The more I tried, the more certain he'd be that I was trying to worm my way in to gather evidence against him.

I turned away from the view and began trudging up the hill. If he really knew anything about the Maxwell picture I'd never find out unless I could figure some way of persuading him that I wasn't working with the police. Show him my passport? Get an upright antique dealer like Reggie West to vouch for me? Bring out a letter from the police disowning me? The more I thought about it the more hopeless it seemed, and in the end I gave it up.

At four, I drove over to Villiers's house. The door was opened by his wife, the human bindweed. She was wearing a light, short-sleeved cashmere pullover and a soft tweed skirt. They clung snugly and emphasized her not-inconsiderable curves. I was struck again by the smooth cream and roses of her complexion, set off by dark hair and eyes.

"Good afternoon, Mr. Eddison," she said, and both smile and voice seemed to reach out and twine around me.

I said, "Your husband told me to drop by."

"That's right. Please come in." She led the way into the small sitting room, adding, "Charles isn't here. He said he'd be late. I hope you don't mind waiting."

"Not at all."

We sat down and she managed to get her chair so close to mine that our knees touched.

"I know Americans aren't really much interested in tea," she said. "Isn't this what you call the cocktail hour? Perhaps you'd like some sherry?"

"No, thanks."

"I saw the piece in the paper. What a shocking thing to happen. Were you terribly frightened?"

I thought I caught a faint, mocking undertone. It was the way she talked to her husband, and so when I replied I kept it cold.

"It wasn't all that frightening. They attacked me and I

fought them off until the cops came."

"Yes, I suppose you are accustomed to frightful happenings in America. There's so much more violence there."

She leaned towards me and I got a hint of her perfume, a flower scent spiced with the warmth of her body.

"I sometimes think you're more vital than we are," she went on. "We don't like things to interrupt our peace and quiet. We've become rather exhausted. I often feel I'd like to get away—go to America. I've never been there. It must be very exciting."

There was something soothing about her voice. She spoke and moved in slow motion, as it were, and it had the effect of suspending time.

"You'd probably enjoy it," I said. "Attractive women are always welcome."

She smiled. "I didn't realize Americans were so gallant." She bent still nearer, touching my knee with her fingers. "You know, Mr. Eddison, I'm glad you got that painting."

"Instead of your husband?"

"I know it must sound terribly disloyal. But Charles can sometimes be overbearing, and he likes having his own way. I rather enjoyed seeing someone stand up to him."

"You did, eh?"

"Are you going to trade it to him, after all? Or sell it?"

"I don't know."

"I think I should warn you that Charles hasn't any money. He likes to act as if he had, but then. . ."

I had to lean towards her to hear, for her voice had grown throatier and softer.

"He impresses people by his acting. There isn't much underneath, you know. It's mainly bluff."

"Why are you warning me?"

"Because I rather like you, Mr. Eddison." Our faces were very close. I could see the fine grain of her skin, delicately lined at the corners of the eyes, and the moist fullness of her lips. "And I don't much like him," she added. She looked unblinkingly at me. "He's only half a man. Not even that. Bluff. Do you understand?"

Whoa! I said to myself. This is the approach direct if I ever had it.

Yet I couldn't quite bring myself to draw away. I said, "Yes, I understand."

"Well, then—"

And suddenly I found that I was kissing her. Her kiss was in character, slow and lingering, while supple as an octopus she entwined me. She ended up on my lap. Luckily, the chair was a sturdy one.

With her lips close to my ear, she whispered, "Shall we go upstairs?"

"Now, wait a minute—" I muttered.

"There's nothing to worry about. Charles won't be home for an hour." Her tongue moved delicately in and out of my ear. "I've never had an Indian. Come and show me. . ."

That switched me off. I would have had to be petrified not to have had some response up to that point although I was anything but taken with her, but I knew just what she had in mind and it was a game I didn't want to play, the dark-skinned savage ravishing the defenseless white woman.

I stood up and set her gently on her feet. There was no sense in rousing her anger by a harsh rejection. I didn't need any unnecessary enemies, and in fact she had already proved an ally by telling me that her husband was broke.

"You're very desirable," I said. "However, my religion forbids me to possess any woman unless she has first gone through the Great Purification Ceremony."

She gazed at me in astonishment. "What? Really?"

"That's right."

"What is it?"

"Ah," I said, racking my brains. "Yes. Well, the squaws

119

first spend three days in prayer lying beneath buffalo robe blankets. Then they undergo sweat-baths and ritual tortures. And so on."

"How utterly fascinating," she said.

Before she could go on, I put in, "I'll take that drink now, if you don't mind. Can I have whisky instead of sherry?"

"Certainly."

She straightened her dress and patted her hair before going to pour out a good slug for me and a sherry for herself. I raised my glass to her.

She sat down on the sofa and looked speculatively at me.

"You know," she said, "I don't think I'll ask you whether all that stuff is true or not. You're a very interesting man."

"And you're a very charming woman, Mrs. Villiers," I replied.

"You don't think there are times when religion can be ignored?"

I grinned at her and she gave me a smile that was all at once quite different from her usual languid one, being open and merry.

"You're making it very difficult for me to resist," I said. "But as a visitor I think it's wiser all around if I stick to the ways of my ancestors."

"Perhaps you're right. I sometimes wish—"

She stopped, and I saw that she was looking past me. Villiers stood in the doorway. I hadn't heard him come in and I couldn't help wondering how long he'd been there. I was also very glad we hadn't gone upstairs. I got up slowly.

"You're back earlier than I expected," Mrs. Villiers said.

He grunted. "Good afternoon, Mr. Eddison. Sorry I kept you waiting."

His voice was not quite as loud as usual.

"Not at all," I said. "I've enjoyed talking to your wife."

120

"Yes, she can be a most engaging hostess."

He had an odd expression on his slab-cheeked face, certainly not suspicion, more like annoyance, and I put it down to the fact that he didn't want his wife to be friendly with anyone. Not surprising, if she was telling the truth about him. A man who can't satisfy his wife generally sees threats everywhere.

I changed the subject. "You said you might have something to show me."

"Quite so." He glanced at his wife but she only looked coolly back at him and sipped her sherry. After a moment, he said, "Come into the next room, Mr. Eddison."

We went into the panelled room. He didn't bother asking me to sit down, but moodily pulled an envelope out of his pocket.

"I hope these will satisfy you that your painting is in fact a copy," he said.

He handed me two photographs, taken with a Polaroid camera and still curly. They were of landscape paintings, one an oil, the other a watercolor, both evidently late Victorian, competent, even pretty.

"What's this supposed to prove?" I asked

He gave me a folded piece of paper. It was a handwritten note on plain stationery.

> I certify that the small oil painting of a landscape in the Dutch style, sold by me to Mr. George Puncheon of Chaworth, was originally purchased from Mrs. James Croft as the work of her grandfather, H. T. Maxwell. The attached photographs are also the work of Maxwell, both painted in the late 1870s.
>
> Arthur Thompson

"Well?" Villiers said.
"Well; what? Very interesting."
"What further proof could you want?"

121

"I don't know. I'll have to give it some thought."

He said, with a return to loudness, "You're a very difficult man to convince, Mr. Eddison."

"I guess maybe I am. That's why I'm still in business."

He jammed his hands into his jacket pockets. "I call it a damn bad show. I've done everything I said I would. I have been as fair as anyone could ask. Now I'd like to know what the hell you're playing at."

"I'm not in the habit of playing at anything connected with my business, Mr. Villiers," I said, giving the words an edge. "Pictures may be a game for you, as they are for a lot of collectors, but for me they're three meals a day and rent. I bought that painting with a definite idea of what I could do with it. You've been chasing me to get it, and you've been chasing hard. It may very well be only a copy. I happen to like it. What's more, I've got a customer in the States who will probably like it. I have to weigh what's best for me, not what's best for you."

I folded up the paper and put it away. I said, more amiably, "I'm sure this seems very tough to you. But I assure you, I'm not just trying to dangle a bait in front of you in the hope of raising the price. You've already made me a good offer of a swap—the Rowlandson drawing. I haven't forgotten about that. You've done your best to prove to me that my painting isn't worth much, that you only want it for sentimental reasons and because it might be nice to have in your collection. Okay, you've made all your points, Now, all I'm asking you to do is give me a breathing space in which to consider all sides of the matter."

"You've already had plenty of time."

"I haven't. I've got other things on my mind as well as this affair. Something personal, much more important to me than whether or not to trade you a painting."

"How long do you expect me to wait?"

"Not long. I'll phone you some time on Monday."

"Monday—!"

"That's it. You've been very patient. Surely you can wait a little longer."

He glowered at me. But I was now being so quiet and polite that he had nothing to work against.

"I don't see that I have much choice," he said. "But I still think it's outrageous."

"Life's like that," I said, winningly, and headed for the door.

There were six other guests at the dinner table and I still hadn't caught all their names. I knew that the husky-voiced woman next to me was either Mrs. Dance or Mrs. Dunce. Her husband, sitting across the table near its foot, was a tanned, bald, fit-looking man wearing one of the most magnificent cashmere jackets I had ever seen. In the course of a brief chat with Mrs. Dance, or Dunce, before dinner I had seen her swallow down three straight whiskies one after the other; she was now drinking hock as if it were water while picking vaguely at her fish. Opposite me was a man with a Roman profile, a touch of silver at his temples, and fine, blue eyes. His name was Carmichael. When I had met him, he had said, "Oh, ah, yes, quite," and nothing else. His wife, a thin woman with lacquered hair, sat at the foot of the table opposite my hostess. The other couple were named something like Bettleah, which didn't seem probable. He was a shrivelled old man with a wrinkled, foxy face, and she was plump, comfortable, and dowdy.

They had all been sympathetic when we met and most of them had said something condoling about my battle with the skinheads, but nobody had asked any questions and I wasn't sure whether to put it down to politeness or apathy. Now, however, Mrs. Dunce, pushing over her glass so that I could refill it, said hoarsely, "I understand you're a Cherokee. I have an American cousin who's given a lot of money to the Cherokee college in Talequah. Is that where you went to school?"

"No," I said. "We moved away from Oklahoma when I was a kid and I grew up in Connecticut."

"Where?"

"Hartford."

"My husband has a relation in Greenwich, Connecticut. Same name, Dance. Do you know him?"

"I'm afraid not."

"They keep an enormous stable, but of course they're much richer than we are. Do you ride?"

"I can stick on a horse if I have to."

"Like polo?"

"I'm going to see some tomorrow with Colonel Hatch."

"You know Tom, do you? A charmer. Known him for years. You'll see us tomorrow, then. We never miss a game."

Mr. Bettleah, who sat on her other side, leaned forward and said, "Have you known Colonel Hatch long, Mr. Eddison?"

"No, I only met him—" I had to stop and think, for it seemed ages ago, "yesterday. But I must say I liked him a lot."

His face puckered. "He's a very likeable man. We have little wine tastings once a month, he and I. Do you like wine, Mr. Eddison?"

"Yes, very much."

"Tom is a claret man, while I am rather more attracted to the burgundies. My wife doesn't drink wine, it disagrees with her. So we two old men meet over a bit of bread and cheese, generally at his house. He has some good things in his cellar, and I bring over a sampling of whatever I can find in mine."

He smacked his lips. Mrs. Dance growled, "Men must have toys to play with. Tell me the truth, Simon, can you really distinguish one wine from another?"

"Only with the greatest difficulty," he replied.

"I don't believe it."

Mr. Carmichael, opposite me, said, "I like anything with alcohol in it. The more the merrier, what, what?"

"I dare you to prove it," Mrs. Dance said, ignoring him. "Come on, Simon. Guess the next wine. Don't let him see the label, Julia."

Mrs. Puncheon, rearing back as if before mildewed fodder, said, "Oh, I really don't think—"

"Don't be such a spoil-sport," said Mrs. Dance. "Or are you afraid, Simon?"

He shook his head good-naturedly. The maid, at a word from Mrs. Puncheon, brought a bottle of wine from the sideboard and poured a little into his second glass. He poked his small, red-tipped nose into it, took a mouthful and savored it, and said, "Well, of course, it's a claret. I'm not very good with clarets."

"Ah. Excuses!" cried Mrs. Dance.

Everyone else had fallen silent. Mr. Dance, his eyes twinkling with amusement, absent-mindedly twisted a button on his delicious jacket. Carmichael's mouth hung a trifle open. Mrs. Puncheon looked worried, not wanting one of her guests to be embarrassed, I suppose. Little, dumpy Mrs. Bettleah, if that was her name, wore a fond, complacent smile.

The old man went on, "However, as it happens, I had some of this very wine to drink not three weeks ago. I can therefore declare it to be a '61 Beychevelle, and very good it is, too."

"Well done," said Dance. "There you are, darling. Let it be a lesson to you to keep clear of things you don't understand. Stick to horses."

Mrs. Dance didn't seem at all put out. "I still don't believe it," she said.

"Simon's quite right, though," said Mrs. Puncheon, looking relieved. "It is a Beychevelle."

"I think that was a great demonstration," I said. "I envy you, Mr.—ah—I'm sorry, I didn't get your name."

"Bentley."

"I admire anyone with an ability like yours."

"Nothing to admire," he said, looking pleased. "It's the

126

result of diligent cultivation of a minor talent. I retired some years ago and I haven't anything better to do with my time."

Dance put in, "It's a vanishing art, Simon. People nowadays aren't interested in cultivating anything more demanding than a taste for pornography. We're in the age of the lowest common denominator, and the lower and commoner, the better. In another twenty years, if the unions and the socialists have their way, any man with a palate for wine or art will be taken out and shot."

"I won't live to see it," Bentley said.

"Surely you're exaggerating," said Mrs. Carmichael. She inclined her tall, lacquered coiffure towards Dance. She had one of those painfully earnest faces which always remind me of Leagues and Committees. "I should have thought English working people have always shown a desire to better themselves. According to a survey I read recently, attendance at museums is higher now than ever before in history."

"I never trust surveys," said Dance, picking up his knife and fork. "I rely on my own observation. I find I'm generally right."

The plates had been changed and the next course, over-done roast beef, had been put before us. The wine was poured and I tasted it. Even I could tell that it was very good.

"If what you describe ever happens," I said, "this village will suffer, Mr. Dance. I've already run into a lot of people here who are anything but levelled. Mr. Bentley knows wine, and so does Mrs. Puncheon, obviously. Colonel Hatch is a connoisseur of whisky as well as other good things. I've met a first-rate painter who's going to be important some day when they discover him. And I've met a man with one of the best small collections of Dutch art I've every seen. If I could find all that in an out-of-the-way village in a couple of days, I suspect it'll be a long time before the levelling takes effect."

"Americans can always find more good in England than we English can," said Mrs. Dance, helping herself to another glass of wine. "And it's shaming how you always know so much more about our history than we do. I can't even remember how many wives Henry VIII had."

"Who's the man with the collection of Dutch art?" Dance asked.

"I think Mr. Eddison must mean Charles Villiers," said Bentley.

"Really? I shouldn't have guessed."

"He keeps his collection safely out of sight," Bentley chuckled. "Inside a set of false panels in the drawing room. But evidently Mr. Eddison won his way into the sanctum."

"He's got some fine pictures," I said. "We may have a deal cooking. He wants to trade me something for a painting I own."

"I'd keep a sharp eye on him if I were you," Dance said. "I won't say he's dishonest, but he's not very scrupulous."

"I trust him about as much as I would a gondolier with water wings," I said. "I've been a dealer for quite a while and I've lost my innocence."

Mrs. Puncheon said, "Won't you have some more cauliflower, Mr. Eddison?"

It occurred to me that maybe she didn't want her friends discussing each other at her table. The same thought must have struck Bentley because he put in, "I must tell you a touching story about innocence. It concerns Tom's father, old General Hatch. He was something of an amateur magician, and whenever he visited Tom and Ruth he brought along some trick or other to show young Harry. When the General died, they took Harry to the funeral. I suppose he must have been five or six, then. There was an honor guard, and when they fired off the salute, Harry screamed out, 'Now he's going to jump out of that box!' "

We all laughed, and the conversation went on to other things.

128

After the cheese—which the English serve following dessert for some opaque reason of their own—Mrs. Puncheon rose and said to Bentley, "Simon, I'll leave the gentlemen in your care. You know where the cigars are."

She ushered the other women out, and Bentley got a box of cigars out of a sideboard and then took her chair at the head of the table. Port and brandy were already there, and as we helped ourselves I couldn't but think how civilized a custom this was.

Dance had moved up to sit next to Carmichael, and now said to me, "I wouldn't dream of meddling in your affairs. I hope you understand that I said what I did about Villiers out of nothing more malicious than concern for a stranger."

"I took it that way."

Carmichael had been lighting a cigar, and he said, "Oh, ah, Villiers, that's the chap with the pretty wife. Met them at the Conrans, I believe. In plastics, isn't he?"

"That's right. Shall I tell you something about the fellow? One of my little projects is a furniture plant near Gloucester. Villiers's factory makes moulded plastic, and my manager had taken quite a large order for a rather dashing chair we'd designed, something like a mitten if you follow me—" he held up a cupped hand to illustrate, "and we gave Villiers the order for the plastic shells. Not an enormous amount of money, you understand, but since the fellow was a neighbor I thought I'd pass him the business. Came the day of reckoning, I mean delivery day, and it came and went without the stuff turning up. My manager phoned his shop and got nothing but excuses and so he put me on to it. I don't generally like to interfere in these matters. Anyway, I phoned and Villiers apologized and asked if I'd come over and see him. 'I was about to ring you,' he said. Right; I went round and he had a chap in his office whom he introduced as his works manager. 'Now, then,' he said—you know how he booms, do you?—'I'd like you to tell Mr. Dance what you've done, you sod.' The manager, a poor thin sort of stick, confessed to me that he had made a mistake in the specifications and the whole order had gone wrong. They'd be two or three weeks late with it at the least.

"Naturally, I was bloody cross. Then Villiers said to the chap, 'You're finished, pack up your things.' He then apologized all over again, and of course I accepted it since he'd fired the chap. I couldn't ask him to do more. It meant a penalty for us and a bloody nuisance all round, and the trouble was, you see, that I hadn't given him a penalty clause in his contract, thinking he was a gentleman and a neighbor and all that.

"But a couple of years later, I found out what had happened. A man who used to work for Villiers came to work for me, in a little shop I've got that turns out office machinery. He was a real efficiency expert and I eventually put him in charge of the place. We were chatting one day, and he came out with the whole story. It seems Villiers had lined up a really big order with United Motors, making moulded plastic interiors for cars. So he just shoved my bit of an order aside and took on the other. Then, when he saw he was in a spot, he threatened his works manager with the sack if he didn't take the rap by pretending to have messed things up. The whole thing, the scene in his office, was just an act for my benefit, you see."

"I say," said Carmichael. "That was damn clever."

"It was damned indecent," Dance retorted, but without heat. He was evidently inured to Carmichael's idiocy. "Needless to say, I wrote Villiers a stiff note and I don't see him now when we meet, which isn't very often anyway."

"I can understand you'd be annoyed," Bentley said. "I find Villiers pompous but harmless. But then, I've never had any business dealings with him."

I said, "I wonder if I can ask you gentlemen something. You were all friends of Mr. Puncheon's, I take it. Perhaps you know the painting I bought at the auction on Thursday, a copy of a Dutch landscape?"

"Frankly, I never paid much attention to George's pictures," Dance said. "We were generally concerned with more practical things."

Bentley put his fingertips together. "I imagine I must have seen the picture you mean, but I can't bring it to mind. I know of it only because Julia told me you bought it. And she said it fetched quite a bit more than she anticipated. I must confess I was puzzled. Is it a good painting?"

"I like it."

"Then I wonder why Sotheby's refused to sell it?"

"The fact that I like it and that I have a customer for it doesn't mean it's good in the sense that it's a fine work of art, or that it would necessarily bring in enough money for a big firm like Sotheby's to handle it. It just happened that there were several of us at your local sale who wanted it and competition can do funny things to prices."

"You couldn't be righter," said Dance. "The lifeblood of an economy. Although you'd never believe it to listen to the socialists."

I went on, to Bentley, "So I don't suppose you know anything about the picture—where Puncheon bought it or what he paid for it?"

"Not a clue."

I sighed, and gave myself a little more brandy as consolation.

"I can't help being curious about Puncheon's death, too," I said. "They never did find out what he was doing at the castle that night, did they?"

"I suspect he was meeting someone," Carmichael said, waving cigar smoke aside. "A woman. That's my theory."

Dance blew out his lips. "So you said, John. Rubbish!

131

Just because he and Julia quarreled over the CPRE non-sense—"

"Oh, yes, I've heard about that," I said.

"She didn't want him to pull down Pellet Lane and begin quarrying," said Dance. "Well, now she's got her way. I've tried to buy the property from her. I wouldn't mind developing it myself. Got a few ideas. Not a quarry, mind you, that's short-sighted. Once you've taken out all the stone, where are you? You're left with a hole in the ground. No, I should fix the place up if it were mine and divide it into flats. But Julia won't sell it. For one thing, she has some notion of loyalty to her family."

"Ah," I said. "Sterlet. That's right, he's her cousin."

"You've met him?"

"Yes. Quite a character."

Bentley said, "It's not just that she thinks he ought to be allowed to go on living there. She has an attachment to the house. Her grandmother and Donald Sterlet's were sisters. They were Huntercombes, and the two families had several connections. I don't know whether there are other Sterlets in England. Donald's the last of the line here in Chaworth, anyway."

"I see. No wonder she and her husband disagreed over the property."

"Disagreed?" Carmichael uttered a guffaw. He sat erect, cigar in one hand, a glass of port in the other. He looked like the façade of some noble but tenantless building. "She couldn't stand the man. Nor could I. Never liked him. Felt there was something pushy about him. Just the sort of fella to go meeting a woman in the middle of the night."

"I hardly think the theory will hold water, John," Bentley said, patiently. And turning to me, clearly changing the subject, he said, "I hope you'll enjoy the polo tomorrow. Have you ever seen a game?"

"No."

"Well, you'll have the best of interpreters for it, with

132

Tom Hatch. He used to play, of course, when he was a young officer. And after India got its independence, in '48, and he came home again he still played now and then although he was nearing fifty. Lord Knowell always found him a mount, didn't he, Peter?"

Dance nodded. "I've heard they were jolly glad to get him, too, he was a very daring player. I only saw him play once, and he rode like a demon. After he gave it up, Knowell hired him as the club's polo manager for a couple of years."

I had been counting on my fingers, and I said, "That means he's over seventy now."

"Quite right," Bentley said.

"He sure doesn't look it."

"He's extraordinary. Once, in the Western Desert his regiment was pinned down under heavy fire. Tom got up, tucked his stick under his arm and said, 'All right, chaps, I've had enough of this. Let's persuade them to pack it in.' He then walked calmly towards the enemy position in the face of machine gun and mortar fire and after a second or two his men followed him. They rushed the position and took it."

"That was taking a chance, wasn't it?" said Dance.

"He fought the way he played polo. Didn't mind taking cold-blooded chances. He had a reputation for ruthlessness, too, you know. It was said he never took prisoners."

"I wouldn't have guessed that," I said.

"No, he doesn't show much. For instance, after Angela's death only his closest friends knew what he felt."

Bentley sighed and decisively thrust his chair back.

"Well, gentlemen," he said—and I held my breath. He wasn't really going to say it? But he did—"Shall we join the ladies?"

That made my evening.

We went into the big sitting room and found the ladies drinking coffee, all but Mrs. Dance who was working on a large whisky. We men had some coffee. I was beginning to feel the need of it what with a drink before dinner, a good deal of wine, and two brandies, but the others didn't seem greatly affected. Carmichael never showed anything anyway; Dance, although he turned plum-colored, obviously had as large a capacity as his wife's; as for Bentley, I guessed he tasted rather than quaffed.

We broke into small groups and there was a lot of casual chat. At one point, Mrs. Puncheon, who like a model hostess was spending ten minutes in conversation with each group, came over to me, thus freeing me from Mrs. Carmichael who had been telling me in grave detail about the work of the Chaworth Branch of the Society for the Promotion of Ethical Standards in Television.

Mrs. Puncheon said, almost shyly, "Mr. Eddison, when you spoke earlier of an artist who will some day be famous—"

"I was talking about Sterlet," I said.

"I wondered. Do you really think he has talent?"

"I do. In spite of his peculiar behavior—"

"I warned you you might find him eccentric."

"To tell the truth, we had a slight disagreement. But never mind that, the fact is I do think he's a real painter."

She sighed. "I can't understand his work myself. A great deal of modern art is so very strange, don't you think? But perhaps you don't. It's closer to your generation than to mine. Still, I'm pleased to hear what you think. Since art is your business, after all, you must know what you're talking about."

"I'm an antique dealer, not an art dealer," I said. "You mustn't take what I say as gospel. But if I can ever settle things with him, I'll buy one of his paintings myself."

Soon after, the Bentleys got up to leave, and the rest of us followed suit. We stood in the hall saying our goodbyes, the Dances remarking again that they'd see me at the polo game, and Mrs. Bentley, who hadn't said a word to me all evening, shaking my hand vigorously and urging me to ring up very soon so that I could see her garden at its best. Mrs. Puncheon said, "Oh, just a moment, please, Mr. Eddison, I want to tell you something," so I waited until the others had gone.

She said, "You *are* still trying to find out something about the painting you bought?"

"Yes. I think I know now where your husband got it, but it would be useful if I could find out how much he paid for it or what he thought it was."

"Yes, I see," she said. "George kept a catalogue of his collection. I don't know exactly what he wrote in it, but I believe it contained a record of all his purchases. I remembered it after I spoke to you on the phone this afternoon."

"That would be great," I said, eagerly. "Where is it?"

"Charles Villiers has it. He took it when he took the paintings, in hopes that it might be useful to the Sotheby people."

"And he never gave it back?"

"No. Well, you see," she said, "I had no particular use for it." She drew herself up, the thin nostrils quivering, the long, homely face taking on an unexpected dignity. "I wasn't very interested in my husband's collecting," she said. "I don't know what your experience has been but mine is that passionate collectors give up some of their humanity. The things they want sometimes become more important to them than people."

I thought I understood what she meant. I remembered Carmichael saying, "Disagreed? She couldn't stand the man." It must have been a marriage without much love. Puncheon had collected more than paintings and giant statuary. He had tried endlessly for bargains, in property, reputation and position. And she herself may have been collected along the way, for her house, her social position or her money, a useful object, another bargain.

135

She said, "I'm sure if you ask him Charles will show it to you."

"Fine," I said. "I'll do that. Thanks very much."

I was willing to take any bet that getting Villiers to show me that catalogue was going to be about as easy a job as trying to open an oyster with your pecker.

Somewhere around the middle of the morning I was ruminating among the pages of the *Observer*—much thinner and more genteel than any American Sunday paper—when Jill phoned. "Bob darling, are you all right?" she said.

"Of course I'm all right," I answered, puzzled by the urgency in her voice.

"I've just seen the local newspaper."

"Oh, that. Nothing to it."

"You mean it isn't true."

"It's true all right, more or less, but I wasn't much hurt."

"I'm so glad. Aunt Grace and I were away yesterday—I drove her to Wells for a Women's Institute do—and we got back late last night. It must have been horrible for you. I wish I'd known sooner. You must have wondered why I didn't phone."

"Honey, don't think twice about it. How are you?"

She hesitated. "I'm all right, Bob," she said, in a small voice.

"You haven't decided yet?"

"I want to come and see you. Shall I come over now?"

"That sounds ominous."

"It wasn't meant to."

I didn't know whether to dare feel cheerful or not.

"I'm supposed to go see a polo match this afternoon with a local man," I said. "I can cancel it and we can spend the day together."

"Don't cancel it. Could I come along? I've seen one polo game and enjoyed it."

"Great. I know Colonel Hatch wouldn't mind. Come now, and we'll take a walk somewhere and then have lunch together here. The food isn't bad. Okay?"

"It sounds lovely."

After she hung up I went downstairs and started pacing. I must have covered three miles in the lounge before she arrived. I looked up suddenly and there she was, fresh and dewy and bright, like a brand-new morning. It was as if I had just that minute fallen in love with her. She seemed more alive than anyone else in the world; I felt as if I had been walking in Flatland all this while and had now broken through into a new dimension.

I took her in my arms the way you accept a delicate piece of old lacquer, not believing my luck at being able to embrace this marvelous girl. Nothing else mattered right then. I postponed any apprehension.

After a bit, she murmured, "Everyone's looking at us."

And in fact, a nice white-haired old man was grinning at us in an approving way over the top of his *Times*, and Albert, the roundfaced maitre d'hôtel, was smirking from the cigarette machine he was filling.

"All right," I said. "We'll go for a walk."

I drove her out to the common. It was nearly noon and there were already cars parked and people setting out their picnics to take advantage of the sun. Here and there, young men lay stripped to the waist, pillaged corpses slowly browning. Next to each car there was a folding chair, a portable stove with a tea-kettle, and a basket full of sandwiches. Young bullocks forsook their grazing to come and stare with wondering, liquid eyes at the intruders. An occasional pony trotted over to accept sugar. Fathers solemnly bowled cricket balls to their small sons. Girls fled screaming together when no man pursued. A couple of kites soared overhead like high spirits.

138

Abandoned newspapers snapped their pages desperately in the breeze, their clamor of the day's disasters unheeded.

We skirted the cars and walked to the edge where the ground dropped sharply so that we seemed to be suspended over the valley. Most of the people stayed near their cars, as if fearful they might be caught without transportation in case there was an earthquake or the Comanches attacked. Far off to the right, I could see a few kids clambering around on the castle walls, with their parents below motioning to them to come down. Their voices were no more than a distant chirping. We were as good as alone, with five hundred yards between us and the nearest group.

We stood holding hands for a while, looking over the green depth and blue distance, and then sat down on the turf.

I said, "I'm not going to ask you anything after all. I'm just glad to be with you."

She looked earnestly at me and said, "I love you, Bob."

"That's good. I can understand nice, simple, declarative sentences."

She put her hand on mine. "I realized how much when I read that newspaper story. I suddenly asked myself what I'd have done if you'd been badly hurt. No, don't say anything yet. I want you to tell me all about what happened, but not now. Now, all I want to say is that I will marry you."

A great wave of astonished joy welled up in me.

"Do you mean it?" I said, foolishly.

She grinned. "I'd better, hadn't I?"

I put my arms around her and kissed her. "Okay," I said. "When? Tomorrow?"

"It can't be quite that quick here, darling. I've never asked you about your religion. Are you—do you mind a church wedding?"

"I don't mind anything if you want it. But I'm not a

139

Christian. Does that matter to you?"

"No, of course not. There's another thing." She bit her lip. "Before we set the date, could you—would you mind coming and talking to Aunt Grace?"

"Why? What's the trouble?"

"I think we ought to tell her together, don't you? She gets so frightfully confused. It's going to be awfully hard for her, poor dear. Not just taking it in, that I'm not going to live with her any longer, but the whole idea of my going abroad."

I could see the shine of tears in her eyes. "Don't worry," I said, firmly. "I'll handle everything. For that matter, why couldn't she come to America with us? I'll bet she'd like Connecticut."

Even as I said it, I felt a qualm. Jill smiled gently and said, "That's good of you, darling. Let's wait and see, shall we? When can you come? Can you manage tomorrow? I want to try to prepare the ground tonight."

"I'll come over first thing. Nine o'clock. Even earlier, if you like."

"No, I have to be in school in the morning. Come at one. We'll have lunch."

"I don't know if I can wait that long." I kissed her again, and we got up. "Come on, speaking of lunch, let's celebrate. We'll have champagne with our Yorkshire pudding. That'll give them something to talk about."

I remembered little afterward of our lunch, for I ate and drank only Jill. Soon after we finished, Colonel Hatch arrived. He greeted us warmly, as if we were old friends, and gave Jill an old-fashioned sort of bow as he took her hand. We climbed into his car and drove to Altoncester, branching off on a side road before we got to the town itself. We began passing a high stone wall on the other side of which was forested land. It ran on for a mile or more until we came to a gate with a little stone house beside it, and a neatly lettered sign that said, *Polo today 3:30.* A

140

man stood beside the road selling tickets and he touched his cap to Hatch and said, "Afternoon, Colonel. A fine day," and waved us on.

Other cars were turning into the road and we went in convoy between the trunks of beeches and oaks up to their ankles in a froth of fern. The trees began to thin and I could see a vista of meadows opening in the distance.

"Who owns all this?" I asked.

"It's Lord Knowell's land," said Hatch. "A fine property. Don't imagine it's idle land. He has a large working farm and he harvests the timber in these woods, as well."

We came out on the edge of a wide, level field. At each end were goal posts with fluttering pennons on their tops. The road divided around the end of the field. On the far side, visitors' cars were lining up along the games line and people were setting out rugs or folding chairs. The near side, marked by a sign saying *Members Only,* had a small grandstand and a thatched building. Hatch nodded to the man taking tickets by the roadside and drove into a clearing where other cars were parked.

We followed him towards the building, one end of which was the club-house, the other the bar without which no English building with the possible exception of a Boy Scout hut is complete. Grooms were walking ponies, there was a chatter of voices, and in an open space to one side a few men on horseback were knocking a ball about, their long-handled mallets swinging in showy circles. Hatch was clearly well known and liked; he was constantly pausing to exchange greetings with people. He introduced us to Lord Knowell, a rangy, broad-shouldered man in his fifties, and as we stood talking I heard the beat of a propeller and a helicopter came into view over the treetops. "That'll be Ted," said Lord Knowell, as it settled down a short distance behind the club-house at the edge of another field. I noticed then that there was another chopper already there. It struck me that polo was no game for pikers.

We went to the bar, where, as I might have guessed, Mr. and Mrs. Dance were established. We shook hands and I introduced Jill. I explained to Hatch that I'd met the Dances the night before.

"I met your friend Mr. Bentley, too," I said. "Isn't he a polo enthusiast?"

"He comes occasionally," said Hatch. "Simon's a more contemplative sort. He'll spend Sunday in the garden."

"His wife mentioned their garden."

"It's very attractive. However, Simon won't be digging. He leaves that to Lydia. He'll be reading."

We had a round, which the Colonel bought. Dance said, raising his glass, "One of the advantages of being a member," and when I looked puzzled, explained, "The licensing laws, Mr. Eddison. The pubs are closed at this hour, but we aren't."

Hatch looked at me with twinkling eyes. "You forgot our barbarism in the matter of drinking, Mr. Eddison, when you were telling me how much you liked England."

"Yes, but it's obvious some of you find ways around it," I said.

We went out and took seats in the stands. The players were on the field, and the two umpires in striped blazers cantered out to join them.

I said, "You'd better give me a rundown on the game, Colonel."

"I won't bore you with excessive detail. There are four riders a side. They'll play six chukkers today which last seven and a half minutes each, with three minutes between and five minutes at half time. The object of the exercise is, of course, to hit the ball between the goal posts. I'll explain other things as they come up, but perhaps one thing you ought to know is that a man following the ball on its exact line has the right of way. That's to say, if

142

another player crosses him close enough to be dangerous, it's a foul. There are other fouls, as well, for instance charging in at an angle—"

"They're starting," Jill said, clutching my arm.

I very quickly grew absorbed. The play went from end to end of the field, now the players bunching together over the ball, their sticks clacking, then one man streaking away with his mallet swinging like a sabre and the other after him. The ponies were incredible; it seemed to me that they understood what the play was about and got as much zest out of it as their riders. They had the agility of cats. They could stop short after a wild dash and turn on a dime, and they seemed to know just how to put their riders into position for a stroke.

A public address system had been set up, and a man at the mike kept up a running commentary: "A hard shot by da Silvio, just wide—that was a good back-hander by Ted Darlington—they're running each other off—Williams cleverly blocked by Mark Outcrop—a great shot by James Outcrop from forty yards and that must be a goal—yes, there's the flag—"

A man on foot was waving a large flag from behind the goal posts and there was a polite spatter of applause.

I kept thinking it reminded me of something—the men with their faces sternly set under the peaks of their helmets shouting directions to each other, the flowing movement of the horses, the intent crowd, the turf flying up in clods from the drumming hoofs, the deep blue of the sky above the green—and then it came to me. It was like a medieval tournament, like the mellays described in King René's book. One could imagine the clatter of sticks transformed into the blows of blunted swords on shields. Under this sky, on just such a field, men on horseback had played an equally rough game five hundred years ago.

And it was rough. A scrimmage, with the sticks whipping among the ponies' hocks, and then a man was off with the

143

ball and another galloping on his tail—"A. Bullstone being hard-ridden by Darlington," cried the announcer—a whirling circle of a stick and they had passed over the ball, the blow having missed it; the next instant the pack was upon it, sticks rose and fell, they went thundering off again and all at once a horse was down. It kicked once or twice and scrambled up again, but its rider lay still.

"A nasty spill," Hatch said, calmly. "However, I daresay he'll be all right."

"What about the pony?" I asked.

He looked blankly at me. "It was the pony I meant."

Play had stopped and a car shot out on the field. A couple of men bent over the man on the ground and helped him to his feet. I could see him shaking his head. After a moment, he remounted and the car drove off.

Dance, on the Colonel's other side, said, "Tony over-reached himself last week and fell off. He'd better learn to play on foot."

"He's a damned good man," Hatch said, with just a hint of reproof. "His only shortcoming is that his judgment is sometimes impaired by an emergency, as it was when Ted rode him off."

I glanced at him. I had a feeling that when he was younger it must have taken a hell of a lot of riding to ride him off, whatever that meant.

When the game was over, we strolled around with the Colonel meeting some of the riders. They all had the same kind of hard, confident face and an air of assurance that seems to go with being on horseback. It is one of the mysterious parts of our culture, going back to that early division between the mounted knight and the foot-slogging peasantry which even Rome knew. It invests the horseman with the power that comes from looking down at other people.

Back in the Colonel's car, he said, "Can I persuade you to come and have some tea with me?"

"We don't want to put you to any trouble."

"I assure you, it'll be no trouble. I enjoy company. It'll be rather simple, I'm afraid, just tea and biscuits."

"We'd love to, Colonel Hatch," Jill said. She was sitting in the back seat and she nudged me between the shoulder-blades to shut me up.

Hatch drove sitting erect, as he stood and walked, his big beak like a prow. He wasn't afraid of speed and handled the car as he must have handled horses, lightly but with absolute control.

He said, "I hope you weren't bored this afternoon."

We assured him that we hadn't been. "It's one of the most exciting sports I've ever seen," I said. "As well as being the only one which players come to in helicopters."

He chuckled. "Yes, one or two of them are busy men and find Sunday traffic unendurable."

"Maybe this is naive," I said, "but it seems to me you have to be better than well-to-do if you want to get deeply involved in the game."

He passed a couple of cars, and then said, "It's an expensive proposition to be a patron of the game, certainly. Horseflesh is costly, and since a pony generally plays only two chukkers in an afternoon one has to have quite a stable. But for every rich man who plays, there are half a dozen not so rich. For instance, a young chap from the Argentine whose father owns a ranch—well, he punches his father's cattle and on weekends plays polo. A patron might well take him on to bolster up a team. Then there are others, young army officers for instance, who play for the joy of it. If they're at all good a patron will always mount them. It's a dangerous game, of course," he added wistfully, "but it is grand fun."

"That was why you played," I said.

"Yes, that was why I played. You see, in India in the old days it wasn't an expensive sport. We didn't have all the amenities some of the clubs have here, but we had rather a good feeling of camaraderie, and we always managed to enjoy ourselves."

When we got to his little house, Jill insisted on going into the kitchen with him to make the tea and I had another look at his knick-knacks and pictures. Then we settled cosily in front of the big windows looking out towards the view, with the tea and biscuits and bread and butter on a low table.

"This *is* pleasant," Hatch said. "Most of my cronies are my age. I don't often have young people here except when my grandsons visit me. They're my son Harry's boys."

"Is your son in the army?" I asked.

"Oh, no. It's not much of a career these days. He's an architect. A good one too, I think. You remember, Mr. Eddison, we were talking about the estate on the edge of Chaworth? You should hear Harry on the subject of new mass-produced buildings. He has his own ideas about the future of villages like Chaworth. He complains that we don't build for people but for quick money, and that the English style, evolved over centuries out of the materials and needs of particular regions, should be used as a basis from which to start rather than the bastard international style so dear to modern jerry-builders, pasteboard and plywood boxes. They might do for a warm and sunny climate, say the Costa del Sol, but they're as alien to England as orange trees."

"Harry sounds like a man I'd like to meet," I said.

"I hope you will some day. Why don't you stay on here for a while?"

"I may have to. Jill and I are going to be married and she tells me it can't be rushed."

"Married? That is splendid. May I offer my congratulations? I hope you'll be very happy."

"Thank you," Jill said, but I saw a cloud pass over her face.

"It should be very exciting for you, going to America,"

Hatch went on. "A new country, very big, very lively, full of all sorts of interesting sights. I sometimes think I should like to go. But I'm too old for it. I shall remain stuck in the mud here."

"It's not a bad place to be stuck," I said, motioning to the view.

"No, not bad. It's all I have to leave my son, this view, this bit of land, and some association with the village, or whatever may be left of it. I hope he'll want to settle here some day, when he's my age perhaps. But one never knows, these days."

He was silent for a moment. I felt very moved. The pleasant day we had shared had pulled down, a little, the barrier I had sensed before. I understood more intimately his loneliness and the deep attachment he had to his own ground.

Jill said, "I'm sorry, I'm afraid I have a slight headache."

She did look pale. Colonel Hatch said, with a smile, "We're not accustomed to so much sun, here."

"That must be it," she said, as we got up.

We went out by the front door and stood for a moment or two looking across the common. There were still a good many cars parked down near the road, and the same people now made tea instead of lunch, yelled at the same kids, played the same games.

"You should see it on a fine Whit Monday," Hatch remarked. "It looks like Bournemouth. They even picnic against my gate. Still, that's what a common is for, isn't it?"

A man strolling by touched his hat to the Colonel. I knew that easy, slouching walk and that massive frame.

"Good afternoon, William," Hatch said.

"A'ternoon, sir."

"Lovely weather, eh? I daresay it'll keep fine. We shall have a full moon tonight."

"I shouldn't 'oonder."

"Have you seen Sir Donald lately?" I said, a trifle acidly.

He blinked at me. "Can't say as I 'ave, sir," he replied. He touched his hat brim again, and went on.

As we got into the Colonel's car, I said, "I take it you said all that about the moon because you know what he does at night."

Hatch chuckled, turning the car. "Oh, yes. William's very good at it, too. I shouldn't condone what he does, of course, but his family have lived here as long as mine. I expect he must have some right to the natural livestock. I don't imagine you have poachers in America, eh? With your vast lands game must be plentiful."

"Reasonably so. What does he go for?"

"Rabbits, mostly. The odd pheasant. And a salmon or two from the Severn."

"If I were going to do any moonlighting here," I said, thoughtfully, "I'd use an air gun so's not to draw attention to myself."

"Good heavens, no! The law is very severe in such matters. If William were ever caught with an air gun he'd be liable to six months' imprisonment or a fine of two hundred pounds, or even both. I can't say, of course, but I should think he uses a catapult."

"A catapult?"

"A forked stick with an elastic. Have you never seen one?"

"We call them slingshots."

"An equally good name for them. Perhaps," he went on, "I'd feel less tolerant if I owned a lot of property, but I like to think that perhaps I wouldn't."

He dropped us in front of the King's Head and we shook hands.

"I have enjoyed today," he said. "I hope we shall meet again, Mr. Eddison, and you, too, my dear."

He drove away. I turned to Jill and said, "How do you feel?"

She caught the front of my jacket, and in a fierce whisper said, "Let's go up to your room."

"Up—? What happened to your headache?"

"It's better."

I took her hand and we went into the hotel. I looked around nervously for Mrs. Orchard but she wasn't to be seen. We hurried upstairs.

In my room, she threw herself upon me. We kissed urgently, furiously; we undressed in haste and got into bed. It had been a year and I relearned her body with delight.

A long time later, we lay spent, her head on the crook of my arm. The sun was nearly gone and a golden light came through the curtains turning her skin tawny and glistening from the fine ends of her hair.

I said, "I don't believe you ever really had a headache."

"Mhm," she said.

"Are you hungry?"

"I could manage something."

"We'll get dressed and go down."

I looked at my watch. It was nearly nine.

"Let's not bother with a big dinner," she said. "We'll go to a pub and have a snack."

She sat up. I put my hand on her back, admiring the color of my skin against hers.

"Jill," I said.

She looked over her shoulder.

"It was when Colonel Hatch said that about going to America. That's when your headache started, wasn't it?"

"You're very perceptive, darling," she said. She bent over me and kissed me.

"You're still not sure, are you?"

She raised herself, an arm on each side of my chest, and looked at me earnestly. "Don't keep asking me," she said. "Why don't you just accept it?"

I began to say something and thought better of it. "All

right," I said. "I just want you to be happy."

"I am happy."

"Good. Let's go, then."

We went down trying to look as if we hadn't been upstairs for the last couple of hours. We got out without attracting any particular attention. There was a pub at the other end of the market square, the Royal Oak, and we went into the lounge bar, which was half empty. They had nothing to eat except some packaged pork pies, lumpy with gristle but filling, and we had a couple, eked out with pickled onions and brown ale.

One counter served both the lounge and the public bar. When I went to refill our glasses I looked across into the other, more crowded room. A young man was standing at the counter and our eyes met. I recognized him with a jolt—the leader of the gang I had tangled with in Altoncester. He knew me too, for he grinned and left the bar.

I returned to Jill. "There may be a little trouble," I began.

She stared at me but before I could add anything the door of the lounge opened and the skinhead came in.

I eyed him warily. To my astonishment, there was nothing but friendliness on his fat face.

"You give me a right jab, you did," he said. "Can't 'ardly lift me arm. No 'ard feelings, though. I want to ask you something. Is that true what they wrote in the paper, about you being a Red Indian?"

"Yes, it's true."

"Cor!" he said, shaking his head. "If we'd known we never would 'ave tried to stomp you like what we done. 'E told us you was a Paki. That's why we went for you."

"He?" I said. "What do you mean, he? You mean somebody set me up for you?"

He looked puzzled, and then got what I meant. "Sure. That's why we was waiting. And 'e paid us, too—twenty

150

nicker. But a Red Indian! You wouldn't be a chief, would you?"

"Oh, sure. I'm a war chief. Thunder Cloud, they call me."

"Wow!" he breathed. "That's why you was so fast with that bottle."

It was clear that he would now gain stature from having lost the fight.

I said, "Now you tell me, who's the man who told you to clobber me?"

He gazed at the floor, shuffling awkwardly, and then looked at me almost pleadingly. "I can't tell you that," he said. "I ain't no nark. I only come in 'ere now to tell you we wouldn't 'ave done it if we'd known."

"I understand," I said. "Thanks."

He nodded. "This your bird?" he said, glancing at Jill.

"Yes."

"Smashin'. See you around, then, okay? And no 'ard feelings?"

"No, no hard feelings."

He left me in a fog through which Jill's voice broke. "Bob."

"Eh?"

"Was he one of the boys who attacked you?"

"The one I knocked cold," I said.

"What was that about some man—?"

"That's right, some man put them up to it."

"Why would anyone do a thing like that?"

"I wish I knew," I said.

"Who could it have been?" She took my hand. "I don't understand. You haven't made any enemies here, have you? What's happening? What are you mixed up in?"

"Take it easy, Jill. I'm not mixed up in anything. Somebody must have mistaken me for someone else. I'm sure there's a simple explanation. Look, forget it, it doesn't

151

matter anyway. I'll come and see you tomorrow and talk to your aunt. We'll get things settled and we'll be married as soon as we can. That's all we have to worry about now."

She seemed satisfied and said no more about it. As for me, I wasn't as easy as I made out to be. And long after I had put her in her car and said goodnight, I kept coming back to what the kid had told me, but I could find no answer that would satisfy *me*.

I still pondered it from time to time next morning, although I had other things to think about. Either the skinhead was lying or I had unwittingly made an enemy. I could not imagine anyone who would want to have me beaten up, except, just possibly, either Sterlet or his friend William. Yet they had both had their own brawls with skinheads and I couldn't see them making allies of the boys. Then perhaps the kid had lied to me. If he had wanted to be friendly he might have thought it best to throw the blame on someone else. But why bother to blame anyone? He didn't strike me as the sensitive type. Then why not give me the man's name? I could understand that, all right. These kids might be monsters but they had their code of ethics, as witness the fact that this same kid had refused to tell the police I had stabbed him.

I gave it up. I got dressed in what I hoped were confidence-inspiring clothes, a business suit and a tie, for Miss Trout's sake. I drove to Altoncester to spend the morning in the antique shops.

I had coffee with Reggie West, and I was walking to a large bookshop at the end of the High Street when a motorcycle came up alongside and popped to a halt. Brother Anselm, gathering up the skirts of his habit, jumped briskly off.

"Mr. Eddison! I was just going up to Chaworth to find you," he said.

"Nice to see you again. How'd you know where I was?"

"Detective work. Oh, well, not very difficult. I read the

153

piece about you in the *Star*. I know a staff man on the paper and I phoned him and asked if he could find out for me where you were. You've had a boisterous sort of introduction to Merry England, haven't you?"

"You could put it that way. Got time for a beer?"

"Sorry, no. I have several errands to attend to. But the reason I wanted to see you was to ask if you could possibly come to the priory and have dinner with us."

"That's very nice of you. When?"

"What about tonight? The reason is—well—you see, we take it in turns to cook and tonight's Brother James's turn. He is actually the best cook of the lot, and so we thought—it won't be an elaborate meal in any case."

I couldn't keep my face straight at the mixture of shyness and eagerness in his manner. "Okay," I said. "Tonight. I don't suppose you allow girls in, do you? I'm seeing my friend Jill. You remember, I told you about her."

"Oh, yes. By all means, bring her."

"What time?"

"We eat early, if you don't mind. Say six-thirty."

"Fine with me."

"Good lad." he explained how to get to the house and climbed back on his machine, grumbling annoyance at his skirts.

In my anxiety not to be too early I dawdled too long in the shops, and in consequence had to make a wild dash for Bartonbury. I got to the house in Silver Street a little after one. I pulled my tie straight and went round to the back door feeling as if I were about to make an entrance in a play for which I hadn't learned any lines.

Jill embraced me, and Miss Trout, with a smile, held out her hand. "I hope you've been enjoying your holiday," she said.

I glanced at Jill, who shook her head.

"Do sit down, Mr. Eddison," Miss Trout went on. "Luncheon will be ready in a moment."

The long wooden kitchen table was set. Miss Trout went

to the larder and Jill slipped her hand into mine and whispered, "Aunt Grace doesn't read newspapers. She says they frighten her."

"Have you told her anything about us?"

"I tried, but she didn't seem to take it in."

We sat down, as Miss Trout came out with a platter of cold ham and tongue.

I waited until we were finished eating, meanwhile keeping up a lively narration of what I'd been doing over the past few days. Then, when we were sitting with our coffee, I decided to be blunt.

"Miss Trout," I said, "this may seem strange to you— what I'm about to say—because you may think I haven't known Jill long enough. I mean, I met her a year ago, and we only saw each other for a week or so, and then I've been away all this time and only just came back—"

I stopped, gulped, and decided that if I was going to be blunt I'd better start.

"The fact is," I said, "we love each other."

She beamed at me. "Oh," she said, "that's no surprise to me."

"It isn't? Good. Then you don't mind?"

"Heavens, no. Why should I mind?" She began to get up. "I'll just take some of these biscuits out to Solomon."

"Wait a minute, Miss Trout," I said. "Please sit down. I'm not finished. We want to get married."

"Ah. Very proper." She sank down with an air of satisfaction, and went on, "I understand. Since Jill has no mother, I shall have to give my consent."

"Actually, no, Aunt," Jill said. "I'm quite old enough to marry without your consent."

"It's something else," I said. "I wondered—we wondered whether you could manage on your own. Without her."

"Oh, yes, bless you," Miss Trout said, gaily. "I shall do very well. Why, you mustn't think I'm helpless. And it isn't as if you were going to be a thousand miles away, is it? We'll be able to see each other from time to time."

I said, gently, "Well, you see, Miss Trout, I live a lot

more than a thousand miles away. Three thousand, in fact.''

She stared at me. "I'd forgotten," she said, at last. "You live in North America, don't you?"

"That's right. In Connecticut."

It was as if gauze had been drawn over her eyes. "Yes," she said. "It is a very long way off."

She picked up her coffee cup with a hand that had begun to tremble, and put it down again. "It will be very strange for you, Jill dear. Won't it?"

I said, hastily, "Oh, it's not so strange. It's a lot like England in some ways. I mean, there are stone walls just like Gloucestershire, and plenty of meadows and trees. The roads are narrow and winding. And the people are pretty good, most of them. I mean, we have our share of trouble like any other place. But on the whole, we're trying to solve—"

I gagged and had to stop. In another minute I'd be singing to the music of a Chamber of Commerce string orchestra. That wasn't the issue anyhow. I had shattered Miss Trout and I didn't know how to put her together.

Out of the silence, Miss Trout said, firmly, "I shall have to get used to it, that's all. I shall be quite all right. I have Solomon after all. And perhaps I could visit you."

"Of course," I said. "That's it! By air it's no trip at all, a mere six or seven hours."

"Oh, no. I shouldn't like to travel in an airplane. Heights make me giddy. Perhaps you could come and visit me instead, every now and then. Once a month, perhaps. I shouldn't mind not seeing you more than once a month, Jill."

I opened my mouth and closed it again. Jill jumped up and put her arms around Miss Trout.

"All right, Auntie dear," she said, her voice shaking. "We'll sort it out later."

"Good. That's all settled, then. I suppose there's no hurry, is there?" Miss Trout said, brightly. "I mean, you aren't going to be married tomorrow, or anything like

156

that?" We shook our heads mutely. "I'll go along to Solomon, then. I'm sure you two would like to be left to yourselves."

And out she went with the plate of biscuits.

I said, "She didn't really get it, did she?"

"I don't think so."

"She still thinks we're going to be about as far away as from here to London," I said. "Once a month. Good God! For a minute there I thought she understood. Or does she just withdraw into her fog so she won't have to accept reality?"

"That's not fair, Bob."

"Not fair?" I said, savagely. "How are we ever going to get her to understand, then? Look, why don't we just take her with us?"

"To America?"

"That's right. We can always find some place for her to live."

"She wouldn't live, Bob," Jill said. "She could no more flourish away from this village and this country—than—than—"

"Than you could," I broke in.

She flushed. "I wasn't going to say that."

"No? But it's true, isn't it?"

"No, it's not. Other English girls have married Americans—"

"Other English girls aren't you. It's you I'm talking about. I've been watching you, haven't I, for the last few days, flinching when Colonel Hatch talked about going to a new country, your eyes swimming when you thought about it—even when you said yesterday that you'd marry me you were on the edge of crying. I'm not blind. Sure, you love me. So much, that you're willing to sacrifice the rest of your life to it. The hell with that."

"Bob," she said, with a kind of desperate calm, "don't go on."

I was like a man running madly downhill. "Who are we kidding? It would never work, my pulling you up by the

157

roots and trying to transplant you among the deep-freezes and dry Martinis. And another thing, you don't know what it would be like, being married to me. Somebody like me—Christ, I'm not a person over there, I'm a cause."

She stood up and her chair went over with a crash. "Why are you doing this?" she said. "What do you want of me?"

I could have changed the atmosphere by shutting up and taking her in my arms. But there's a perversity which governs such moments, the impulse which makes you say the one word too much, which turns the caress into a slap.

"I don't want anything of you," I said. "Let's call it off. I'm not going to have your aunt's misery around my neck."

If she had wept, it might still have been all right. But she just looked at me, pale as chalk.

I went blindly out the door. I got into the car and nothing but fragments of words went through my head, aunt's misery, tears, heroes, pull up roots. I knew, in a cold central part of my mind, that I had done it purposely, that I had broken off to save her further laceration. But that was no help for the unhappiness and confusion in which I now floundered.

I found myself at the King's Head without knowing how I got there. I went upstairs, sat down heavily and stared out of the window at the now-familiar view. I hated Aunt Grace, I hated England which had such an anchor in my girl, and I hated myself.

Okay, I thought, when I'd had enough sitting, I'd better get the hell out of here. Back to London, and the first plane home. I began to pack.

I remembered the Maxwell landscape. I had promised Villiers some word by today. Well, I thought, why not swap it for the Rowlandson? I would probably make a better deal that way. And I'd be finished with one more of my problems.

I got it out and studied it again, holding it to the light. It certainly was a fine little painting. The more I looked at it, the more it grew on me. Then I began to think. The trouble was, I had been so wrapped up in Jill, and in following all sorts of odd trails, that I had failed to see what was under my nose.

If Villiers wanted the painting so badly, there could be only one reason. And if I was right about that reason, then there could be only one other reason why Sotheby's had refused the picture.

I began to laugh. Then I picked up the phone and called Villiers's number. His wife answered. I had forgotten that it was Monday, and he was at his plant in Gloucester. She gave me the number and I tried there.

"Villiers here," he boomed.

"This is Bob Eddison. About that painting—"

"Oh, yes. I've been hoping to hear from you."

"Well, here I am." In my smoothest tone, I went on, "Mrs. Puncheon told me something interesting. She said that her husband kept a record of all his purchases, where he got them, their prices, and so on. She said she gave it to you. I'd like to see it."

"I'd be glad to show it to you," he said. "The only trouble is, I haven't it."

"Is that so?"

"Why on earth should I have kept it, Mr. Eddison?" he said. "Julia didn't want it back. And I had no use for it. I threw it away when I'd disposed of the collection for her."

That was reasonable. It was pretty much what I'd expected him to say. But I wasn't finished with him yet.

"I'm sorry," I said, "but I'm still not satisfied about the painting."

"I don't understand." His voice began its usual blustering increase in volume. "What do you mean—?"

"I'll make it plain. All I have to go on is my own feeling about the picture on the one hand, and a note from the dealer on the other. Now, don't get angry, Mr. Villiers, but let's be frank. A note's no proof of anything."

"What?"

"How do I know Thompson isn't willing to do you a favor? I mean, if he owed you something he'd be glad to write you a note, wouldn't he? Come to that, how do I know you didn't write it yourself?"

There was silence for a moment, and then he roared, "Of all the impertinent scoundrels! How dare you?"

I cut in, "That's no answer. If you can't discuss this calmly I'll hang up."

He shut up, but I could hear him breathing. Then he said, "Very well. But your implication—"

"I'm not implying anything. I'm just showing you why a note by itself is no proof of anything."

"Well, what will satisfy you, then?"

"I want to meet Thompson. I have some questions I'd like to ask him."

"I have a question I'd like to ask *you.*" He sounded petulant. "I don't understand why you should be making all this fuss about a nineteenth-century copy."

I decided this was the time to hit him. "I have a theory about the painting, Mr. Villiers," I said. "My theory is that it isn't a nineteenth-century copy."

"Oh?"

"Isn't that interesting? I think it's a genuine seventeenth-century Dutch painting. And what's more, my theory goes that you think so, too."

This time the silence was longer. Then he said, "Why should you imagine such a thing?"

"Now, now," I said. "We're being frank. You've got much too good a collection of Dutch paintings to play the innocent. You can recognize quality better than I can. The more I look at the picture the more I think it's good. So do you. So did Puncheon. Now let me ask you something. Did you ever stop to think where Thompson got the picture from in the first place?"

That seemed to take him aback. "Why, I—no, I didn't."

"You told me yourself he was a crook."

"Yes, but—"

"Enough of a crook to receive a stolen painting?"

"Stolen?"

"That's right. There's a lot of thievery of nice little

160

works of art from small-town galleries and museums. Most of it is never recovered, simply because it's small and relatively unimportant—not Rembrandt, not Goya, just a minor master. You know Thompson, I don't. Would you put it past him to take such a picture if he could get it cheaply enough from the thief? And then, since there might be a bit of a problem disposing of it, stick a label on the back saying it was a nineteenth-century copy? Old dirt and blotted brown ink, that's all it would take."

"But I don't understand," he said. The volume was turned way down, now. "The note I gave you—"

"Also a fake. He's got to protect himself, doesn't he? And when he sold it to Puncheon, he could easily get a hundred pounds for it just as a good nineteenth-century copy—particularly because Puncheon would have his own ideas about it. Well, if Thompson had paid twenty for it, that would be a five hundred percent profit. Not bad for a quick, crooked turnover with no effort to speak of."

"I see what you're getting at."

"Do you? Well, how much did Puncheon pay him for the picture? You saw the record before you threw it away. Well?"

"I don't remember," he said, sullenly.

"I'll bet you do. A hundred?"

"I tell you I don't remember."

"No, and you didn't really ask any questions about it, either, did you? I think you saw right through the label."

"Suppose I did?" He was back to huffing and puffing. "Surely a person like you, a dealer, can raise no objection to my trying to get it cheaply?"

"No, I don't raise any objections. But if it's stolen goods wouldn't you like to know? It might make a difference as far as I'm concerned."

He grunted. "I suppose it might to me."

"I think you and I ought to talk to Thompson together. Once we know what this painting really is, and where it came from, we can get down to business. We can decide between us who gets it. If you can't afford it, we can make

161

a trade—only it'll be a serious trade, based on what the thing is worth."

"What the devil are you proposing? If it were stolen wouldn't you be just as guilty as a receiver—as Thompson himself—if you kept it?"

"And what about you? If you're still hoping to get it cheaply, let me tell you that I'm not going to hand it to you. Either you set up a meeting so we can settle the matter, or I pack up the painting and take it home with me tonight. I've got nothing further to keep me here."

"No," he said. "Don't do that. All right. I'll get on to Thompson at once. But mind you, I can't promise anything. I don't know whether he'll meet us or not. He's still being watched by the police, you know."

"You do your best," I said. "Pick some out-of-the-way spot where he won't feel too nervous."

"I'll ring you back."

"I'll be waiting with bated breath."

I hung up. So I was right. He had as good as admitted that he had recognized it as a painting of real quality. And, of course, he had never taken it to Sotheby's in the first place. Knowing how good it was, even though he had never guessed it might be stolen, he had been afraid it would go to a price far higher than he could afford. So he had held it back and put it in the local auction, where prices would be lower.

The phone rang about ten minutes later.

"I've arranged matters," he said. "It was a little difficult, but at last he agreed to meet us. But it has to be after dark."

"Okay." I remembered something. "I have a dinner date at six-thirty. When is 'after dark'?"

"He suggested midnight."

"A nice round hour. Where?"

"Do you know the ruins of Chaworth Castle?"

"Yes, I do."

"Suppose you and I meet there at midnight, then. If you

162

drive over, you'll see me parked near the gate. He'll be waiting somewhere inside for us."

"In the ruins?"

"He said he'd shine a light to show us where he was."

"Right you are," I said. "The witching hour. I'll see you then."

The Community of the Holy Innocents was a Victorian Gothic house on a hill overlooking the pewtery water of a reservoir. In former days, I suppose it had had extensive grounds but they had vanished under the water and the value of the property had fallen. The house had a kind of tatty grandeur, with its fraudulent battlements, its pointed stained-glass windows, and its front door massive enough to hold back a besieging army.

The brothers themselves were right in character, gray-robed and sandalled. Aside from that, there wasn't much that was saintly and psalm-singing about them. They gathered around the kitchen table joking and laughing, shook hands with me, and jostled into their seats like schoolboys.

There were six of them there—two others, Anselm explained, were away working with a group of young people who were building a youth center. Since I was Anselm's guest, he made the introductions: Simon, the prior, Henry, Matthew, Austen, and, coming to the table with a pot of stew, James, who had done the cooking.

Simon said grace and then began to serve. They passed me a heaping plate, and Matthew, who had a crest of red hair and mild but slightly mad eyes, poured murky cider into my mug.

"Do you sing?" he asked.

I was apprehensive. "Do I have to?"

"No, no," said Anselm. "The joke is, if you don't you will when you've had some of our cider."

It was rough, strong stuff.

"Now and then we 'ave wine, too," Henry said, dreamily. He was the youngest, with several missing teeth and an appealing shyness.

"Somehow, I never think of monks drinking," I said.

Simon smiled. In a lilting voice, he said, "It's a long tradition. The Benedictines and the Carthusians even made their own cordials, very celebrated they were—still are."

Anselm, passing me the bread, said, "I'm sorry your girl-friend couldn't come. I'd hoped to meet her."

"She was busy," I said, curtly.

He glanced at me, catching the strain in my voice, and quickly said, "And have you had an interesting holiday here—aside from your bash-up with the gang in Altoncester?"

"It's been great. I'll be sorry to leave."

"Brother Anselm tells us that you are an art dealer," said Simon. "It must be a fascinating profession, to be buying and selling the creative work of painters."

I said, "It sounds to me as though you don't altogether approve."

"To tell you the truth, I am not sure I do approve. I do not like to think of art as merchandise, like Mr. Smith's cabbages."

"It isn't exactly the same thing. But if artists agreed with you how would they make a living?"

"Yes, yes, I see. There is a point you have. But surely, when the painter is long dead you go on making profit out of his work?"

"All I'm pointing out," I said, "is that a painting *is* a kind of merchandise. Anything people want badly enough and are willing to pay money to own, is merchandise. That doesn't diminish its virtue. Painters, sculptors, even poets, have to sell what they produce, to eat. Haven't you ever wanted to own a painting?"

165

"Oh, yes," Anselm said. "I have. There's a landscape by Seurat in the Bristol Museum—if someone gave it to me, I'd bloody well cherish it, my lad."

"Why would you want a painting?" asked Matthew. "You can step outside and see all the landscape you like."

"True," Anselm answered. "But there's a difference in the way an artist sees things. It's his vision we want, not just the landscape."

"I don't understand that at all," Matthew said, shrugging.

Simon put in, "To come back to what we were saying, Mr. Eddison. You say that being merchandise does not diminish the virtue of a work of art. If a rich man comes to you to buy a painting by—well, say Rembrandt—does he always see the painting? Or does he see it as an investment?"

"I only wish I had a Rembrandt for some rich man to buy," I said. "But you're right, he might see it only as an investment. That doesn't change the painting, though. It remains what it is, no matter how anyone thinks of it."

"But I think then its virtue *has* changed," Simon persisted. "For its virtue is to stir the heart of whoever looks at it, not to make him begin thinking how much it is worth."

I scratched my jaw. I couldn't think of an answer, offhand.

He went on, in the same soft tone, "I once read something by a Chinese philosopher, some chap who lived centuries ago. An essay on art, it was. He said, 'The wise man may own beautiful things but he is not owned by them.' There's the danger with us, today, unfortunately. We cannot simply own. We become the property of our property."

He looked at Anselm, and grinned. "However, if the Bristol Museum gives you the Seurat you may keep it."

"Ooh, thanks very much. I will."

When dinner was over, Anselm took me on a tour of the

166

house. It was furnished very simply, and he explained that they relied on gifts a good deal.

"We have one friend, a man in Cheltenham, who sends us a case of wine from time to time. You remember what Henry said? He'd never tasted wine until he joined the community. He used to be a member of a bicycle-chain gang in Birmingham. We're quite a mixed crew. Matthew worked on a farm. James is a North Country man, used to do something in the wool trade."

"What about Simon?"

"His father was a miner. He educated himself, a very interesting man as you saw."

"I sure did."

He led me into a high-ceilinged room which they had made into a chapel, with unpainted but polished wooden benches and an oak altar with a simple silver cross on it. It still retained its old-fashioned heavy draperies at the tall Gothic windows.

"Do you notice the smell?" he said.

I sniffed. There was a faint spicy odor in the air.

"Incense?"

"No," he said, "we only use incense on high feasts. We don't know what it is. We thought it might be the furniture wax, or the candles, or even the old draperies, but it isn't. It began the day we consecrated the room."

I sat down on one of the benches. I felt sure there must be some perfectly ordinary explanation, but I didn't want to probe into it. The room held a feeling of peace and calm and I preferred to leave it as it was.

Anselm sat down next to me. "You've had some trouble with your girl, haven't you?" he said. "I know I shouldn't ask, but it's the way I'm made. Can't help meself. Do you mind my asking?"

Behind the round steel-rimmed glasses his eyes were warm and sympathetic.

I said, "Why should I mind? We talked about it when we first met, didn't we? She and I are washed up."

"I'm sorry."

Having started, I went on and told him the whole story. He listened with his knobbly hands clasped around one knee, nodding continually.

"It's very sad," he said, when I had finished. "And could you think of no other way?"

"I remember what you said about alternatives," I said. "Maybe there's one somewhere, but I couldn't find it."

He sighed. "Perhaps you shouldn't have made her decision for her. Perhaps her aunt would have adjusted somehow. You never know, do you?"

"No, Miss Trout would never make it in America. It wasn't just her, though. Jill would have pined away. I could see the homesickness beginning when she just thought about leaving. This is where she belongs."

"If you could just put yourself in her place," Anselm said. "Try to see the whole problem from her eyes. Maybe from that viewpoint things would look different."

"Maybe," I said.

He got up. "I'm sorry for you both. I wish there was something I could do to help. Well—would you like to see the rest of the house?"

"Sure, let's go."

I stood up too, and smiled. "You have helped," I said. "I don't know why, but I feel better."

"It's this chapel," he said, with assurance. "It does things for you."

It was growing dark when I left, and the moon was so bright it washed all but a single glowing planet out of the sky. I drove slowly, having about two hours to spare. I stopped near the top of the hill at a pub called the Air Balloon, and had a pint in a noisy, smoky room where I felt very much the stranger, alone and silent in my corner. At closing time I went on to the top and got out of the car and stood for a long time looking over the moonlit valley full of twinkling lights. I thought about Jill and about what Anselm had said. See it from her eyes. That was all very well, but how could I? I couldn't begin to imagine what it was like being English, and a woman. Anyway, it made no real difference, no matter which way I looked at it the answer came out the same.

It got to be late enough, at last, and I headed back for Chaworth. Then, of course, I got lost among the lanes so that it was after twelve when I finally drove across the common to the castle gate, the stones all black shadow and gray silver under the moon. I parked next to Villiers's Jaguar. He got out, pitching away the cigar he had been smoking.

I said, "Where's Thompson? I don't see his car."

"He hasn't one. He'll have taken the local bus from Altoncester. It stops at the crossroads at the edge of the common."

"Have you been inside to see if he's around?"

"I was waiting for you."

"So he may not be here after all?"

"I can't say."

"Okay, let's go inside. You said he'd shine a light."

Our footsteps thudded hollowly on the wooden bridge over the dry moat. Within the walls, shapes were distorted by their shadows and everything looked different, solid walls insubstantial, broken ones darkly solid.

Villiers touched my arm and pointed across the courtyard. In the windows of the chapel where the men had been working yellow light showed, faint against the moonlit reflections on the glass.

"Right," I said. "That must be him."

I led the way to the plank bridge. A wooden gate blocked the way to it and I pulled it open. As I did so, I thought I caught a flicker of movement up on the fallen masonry of the outer walls.

I stared hard, but there was nothing.

Villiers, a little way behind, said, "What's the matter? What are you waiting for?"

"I thought I saw something move up there."

"I don't see anything. Go on."

I put my foot on the planks. I was slow, still looking at the walls, slow enough so that an uneasy movement under-foot, no more than a slight shifting, warned me.

The whole thing fell away with a rush and a clatter, dropping end-first into the gaping crack and crashing on the rocks far below. With its first movement I had twisted myself backward with all my strength. I landed heavily, but safely, among the grassy cobblestones of the court-yard.

I grabbed for breath. The noise of that fall echoed. Still gasping, I made it to my hands and knees, and then up.

"Villiers," I said.

He was nowhere to be seen. Scared. Run off.

Thompson, I thought. It must have been him I saw on the walls. He must have shoved the bridge to the very edge of the crack. But why? What the hell did he want to kill us for? Not us—one of us—the first one on the bridge, who-ever it was.

I was too dazed to think straight. I staggered forward a few steps, slipping on the uneven stones. I saw movement in the dark cave of the workmen's shed and went towards it.

Villiers stood in there, holding a long piece of wood. He raised it and came towards me. In my fuddlement, I thought he looked smaller than usual, or further away than he should be. Then my vision cleared and I realized that I wasn't seeing him but his reflection in one of the sheets of glass standing on end inside the shed.

I swung around, just as he flailed at me. I dodged, and I swear I felt the wind as the chunk of two-by-two went past my head.

I sprang out of reach. His face was set in a mirthless grin, teeth showing in the rictus, the moon in his eyes. He recovered his balance and came for me again. I ran behind the shed looking for a weapon.

An iron crowbar leaned against the wall. I caught it up

and whirled as Villiers came around the corner. I met the swing of his cudgel with the iron and felt the jar. The two-by-two flew out of his hands. I heard him grunt with pain.

He turned and raced for the gate. I heard his feet on the moat bridge and sped after him.

I stopped in the shadow of the gatehouse towers and looked around. He must be somewhere out there on the common.

"Villiers," I said. There was no need to shout. It was utterly quiet and my voice carried on the thin night air.

"Villiers, you son of a bitch," I said. "There isn't any Thompson, is there? I'll kill you if I lay my hands on you, you bastard."

For in a flash it had all come beautifully clear to me.

I strained to listen. If he had gone running across the open common I'd have seen him. He must be lying flat somewhere in the grass. I crossed over the moat hefting the crowbar. I didn't care if he saw me, he couldn't get away. I wasn't thinking about the legal rights and wrongs or what might happen afterward. I just wanted to smash him.

I started walking along the edge of the moat. It was quite deep, and shadowy at the bottom, and he might have scrambled down there to hide. I went as softly as if I were stalking a white-tail, pausing to listen for a rustle of grass or a panted breath.

I heard the slam of a car door. He had outsmarted me.

The lights went on as the engine roared. He shot out in reverse as I stood hesitating. Should I try to chase him? Get to my car? Throw the crowbar at him and break his windshield?

In that second or two, he outwitted me again, and it was nearly the death of me. I saw the headlights growing larger.

Purely instinctively, I dropped flat. I was on the edge of the moat and I rolled down a little way as I fell. The car loomed above me with a rush.

He had planned to catch me with the left side of the bumper. When I just vanished, he couldn't turn fast enough. Both the wheels on the left side went over the edge and the car toppled, still going at full speed. It hurtled down not ten yards from me. With a terrible bang and a shattering of glass it slammed into the bottom of the moat.

I crawled back to level ground. My ears were ringing. I stared down into the moat, shaking my head to clear it. The car lay on its side, half in shadow, half in moonlight, and nothing moved there. I made myself go down the steep bank to it.

It had struck the stone foundation of the castle wall, which formed one side of the moat. The roof and the front had both been driven in. Broken glass glittered. I tried to see inside, but it was hopeless.

A voice spoke above me and I almost jumped out of my skin.

"'e's done for, then, is 'e?"

I recognized William although his face was shaded by his hat.

"I don't know," I said. "I can't tell."

He slithered down to join me. He climbed up on the side of the car and with some difficulty got the door open. He leaned inside and then straightened.

"Dead as can be, I'd say."

He jumped down.

"I'd better call the police," I muttered. "Jesus! What a mess."

"Why trouble? They'll find en soon enough."

"You're crazy. I've got to tell the cops."

We climbed up together. At the top, I panted, "I saw you before, on the wall. Didn't I? You've been here all this time."

"Ar."

"You saw what happened," I persisted. "He tried to run me down."

"I saw it."

I caught him by the arm. "I'll need a witness."

"Somebody's coming," he said. "That'll be Colonel Hatch."

He strode rapidly towards us. When he was closer, I saw that he had pulled on his jacket and trousers over his pajamas. He was carrying a flashlight.

"Who's that?" he called, sharply. "What's happened?" Then, as he recognized me, he said, "Mr. Eddison! What was that crash?"

I pointed. He followed my finger. "Your car?"

"It's Charles Villiers," I said. "He's dead."

"Good God! How on earth—? No, never mind that now. Are you all right?"

"I'm okay."

"We had better go to my house and phone the police."

I said to William, "Well, what about it? I'll need you."

He hesitated and I could guess he didn't want to be asked what he might be doing there at that hour. Then he said, "I'll come."

We walked in silence. At the Colonel's house, he first called the police, explaining that there had been an accident, and then poured me a good big whisky. He glanced at William, who said, "I won't say no to a glass of beer, sir."

Colonel Hatch got him one and gave himself a whisky and then we sat in silence. Hatch cleared his throat several times, and at last said, "You must be badly shaken up."

"I'm all right." I didn't really know how I was, except that by degrees I was pulling myself together. Oddly enough, I kept thinking about Mrs. Villiers. She'd be free to go her own way, now. I wondered how she'd take the news.

After that, there was nothing to be said until the police car drove up. The man who came in first was the detective inspector who had grilled me in Altoncester. With him was another plainclothesman and a uniformed policeman.

The inspector gave me a hard look, and then said, "Good evening, Colonel Hatch."

"Ah, Inspector Preston, isn't it?"

"That's right, sir. What's happened?"

"I think you'd better send one of your men over to the castle," Hatch said. "In the moat, a little to the left of the entrance, he'll find a car."

"This gentleman's car? I really don't see—"

"No, Inspector, not his. It belongs to a man named Villiers, from Chaworth. And you'll find Mr. Villiers inside it, I'm afraid."

Inspector Preston, looking wearier than ever, said to the other plainclothesman, "All right, Batchelor, tell Thorne to drive you across."

He took off his hat, passed a hand over his head, and sat down. The uniformed policeman took out a notebook and pencil.

"Well, sir," Preston said to me, rather drily, "you've been having anything but a quiet holiday. Suppose you tell me what happened."

There was something about his manner that put my back up, just as it had last time. So when I answered, I was curt.

I said, "Villiers tried to run me down. He missed me, and crashed in the moat."

He raised his eyebrows. "I see. Is that all?"

"This man saw the whole thing." I jerked my head at William.

"We'll come to him in a minute. Now, sir, can you suggest any reason why Mr. Villiers would want to kill you?"

"I can suggest one, but you might not believe it."

He folded his arms and sat back. "Mr.—Edgerton, was it?"

"Eddison."

"Yes, sorry, Eddison. I'm just a policeman with a job to do. It'll make things a lot easier for both of us if you just tell me what happened."

"Okay. I have a painting Villiers wanted."

"A painting? What sort of painting?"

"It's an oil, a landscape, about so big." I showed him.

"Where did you get it?"

"At an auction in Altoncester. He was bidding against me. He's been trying to get me to sell it or trade it to him for the last few days. Finally, he proposed that I should meet him at the castle tonight, and he was going to introduce me to a dealer who'd tell me whether the painting was genuine or not."

"And did the dealer show up?"

"Let me ask you something, first. Have you ever heard of an antique dealer named Thompson?"

He shook his head. "Why?"

"Because you're supposed to be keeping an eye on him."

"Never heard of him."

"No, I didn't think you had. There wasn't any such man. It was a trick by Villiers to get me to a quiet place at this hour, and do me in. I can guess he planned to get hold of the painting somehow later on, maybe by simply going to my hotel room and taking it. If you go to the castle you'll see that the plank bridge across the gap in the courtyard has fallen. I think Villiers got there early and put a light in the chapel so I'd think Thompson was there. Then he used a crowbar to heave the bridge forward so that it was just balancing—maybe on a stick or something—expecting that when I walked over it it'd fall with me. I was lucky. I felt it going and was able to throw myself back."

Preston studied me for a moment. "Is that when you suspected him?" he said.

"Oh, no. I still thought the dealer, Thompson, was there somewhere. I thought for a minute that Thompson might have done it. Then Villiers went for me with a piece of wood. I knocked it out of his hand. He ran outside and I followed. He got into his car and drove right at me."

He rubbed his chin. "This painting, is it very valuable?"

"No, it's not. It cost me seventy pounds."

"This is a serious charge you're making," he said. "Are

176

you saying that a man would try to commit murder for a seventy-pound picture?"

"I told you you wouldn't believe me," I snapped. "The man was a collector of pictures. He wanted the painting very badly and I was reluctant to do business with him. You can ask Mrs. Villiers. She'll tell you about her husband."

"Hm. One more thing, Mr. Eddison. Had you been drinking?"

"You want to give me a test? I had dinner with some monks, the Community of the Holy Innocents, near Cheltenham. I had a mug of cider. Then, later, I had a pint of beer. That's all."

"And Villiers?"

"How can I tell? I met him at the castle. For all I know, he was pissed to the ears."

The other detective came in, just then.

"We'll have to cut the body free, Inspector," he said. "It's a proper mess."

"May we use your phone, Colonel?"

"Yes, of course."

"Get a crew up here, then, Batchelor. And phone Dr. Knight-Webb. Then you can go back and take some pictures and check out the car." He turned to William. "Your name, please?"

"William Bullock."

"How did you come to be near the castle at this hour?"

William blinked blockishly. "I like a bit of a walk. There's no law says what time, is there?"

Preston sighed. "Poaching, eh? Well, go on. What did you see?"

"I heard the car drive up, not the first one, the second, with this gentleman in 'er. I was a way down the hill, see, and I thought to myself it might be somebody up to no good. So I come and 'ad a look. I see these two men go into the courtyard. This gentleman stepped on the bridge and down 'er went. Then all the rest just like 'e says, car and all."

177

"What did you do after it happened?"

"I opened the car door and seen it wa'n't no good doin' anything. Then Colonel Hatch come, and us went off and left en."

Hatch put in, "Now, Inspector, you're not going to suggest that Mr. Eddison was guilty of foul play, I hope."

"No, sir, I'm not going to suggest anything. It's my job to collect facts, not make suggestions. The pathologist will have to examine the body, and we'll have to inspect the car. At the moment, I see no reason to doubt Mr. Eddison's story, although there are several points I shall have to check on."

"What do you want me to do?" I said. I was beginning to feel as beat as the Inspector looked.

"How long do you intend to remain in Chaworth?"

"How long do you want me to stay?"

"I shall want to talk to you tomorrow."

"Inspector," said Hatch, "I give you my personal assurance that Mr. Eddison will be available. He has had a disagreeable experience. If you're finished, I suggest that you let him get some rest."

Preston shrugged. "I hope you realize that I'm just doing my duty," he said, stiffly.

"Of course, Inspector. We quite understand."

"Very well. In that case, goodnight." He clapped his hat on, and added, "You'd better tell me where Villiers lived, Colonel. I shall have to have someone break the news to his wife."

When he had gone, walking to the castle where we could see lights and moving figures, William said, "I'd best be off as well."

"Thanks," I said. "It's a lucky thing you were there. Even though your friend Sir Donald thinks I'm with the police—well you can tell him I'm not."

He cracked a grin. "I shall, sir."

When we were alone, Hatch said, "Would you like to stay the night?"

"I don't think so. I just want to rest for a minute or two."

"Your glass is empty. What about another? And I'll join you."

"I want to thank you for helping me just now," I said. "I have a feeling that detective might have dragged me off to jail for the night."

"I hardly think so. What charge could he have held you on? I'm sure he would prefer it to be an accident. So much less trouble that way. And when they have examined the car and the body, they'll be certain of it. You may have to answer some more questions but I doubt there'll be any further trouble."

We sat down with our drinks. I said, "I wasn't altogether frank with him."

Hatch raised his eyebrows, but said nothing.

"Oh, don't misunderstand me," I went on. "Everything that happened at the castle tonight happened just the way I told it. But I could have said a little more about the painting he almost killed me for. You see, I think he did kill Puncheon for it."

That startled him. "What?" he exclaimed. "You're not serious?"

"I am, though. Want to hear about it?"

Hatch brushed his moustache with a finger. "If you feel you'd like to tell me."

"Sure. It might interest you. And I'd like to tell somebody."

"Forgive my saying so, but why not the police?"

"Why should I? It's all conjecture. I haven't any proof. And it won't change anything."

"Go on, then," he said, settling back more comfortably in his chair.

"In the first place, I should amend what I said. I don't think Villiers actually killed Puncheon. He was an arranger more than a doer. I realized it when your neighbor, Mr. Dance, told me a story about how Villiers set up an

179

incident in his factory to get out of delivering some material on time. No, that isn't when I realized it. I really got it tonight when I understood that there wasn't any dealer named Thompson.

"Villiers had sent me to Altoncester to meet Thompson at a pub. I've been told—by one of the skinheads, no less—that somebody paid them to attack me, somebody who told them I was a Pakistani. If there was no Thompson, the only person who could have known where I was going to be at that hour was Villiers."

"Quite so."

"Okay. Now let's go back to the beginning because the whole thing burst on me tonight, bang! just like that. I've been considering the details, and I think I've got it clear, now.

"Puncheon bought the painting I told you about, the Dutch landscape. I thought it was stolen, but that was when I still thought there was somebody named Thompson. I don't know where Puncheon got it, maybe from some junk shop or dealer he did business with, and he thought it was pretty good. The man who *knew* it was good, however, was Villiers. He's got a fine collection of Dutch paintings, and while I don't know what he thought it really was, it's plain to me that he knew it was something well worth having.

"I suspect he tried to get it from Puncheon, perhaps offering him swaps for it. The more he tried, the more Puncheon was convinced that it was an unknown masterpiece, because that's the way his mind worked. So in the end, Villiers figured that the only way to get it was after Puncheon was dead. If he could arrange that death without actually striking a blow, he wouldn't feel guilty. You knew Villiers, didn't you? Wouldn't you say he was a man who liked to get his own way?"

"Yes, I agree. But to have someone killed for a painting—"

"I know. It's twisted. But he was a twisted man. He was an obsessive collector. He was—well, as someone I met

180

earlier this evening would have put it, he was owned by his collection. I don't think anything else existed for him. He was hollow inside, not really a man at all. Never mind how I know that, I know it's a fact. Some men will commit murder for a woman, or for power, or for money. Villiers would for a painting, if it was important enough to his collection."

"Fascinating. Go on."

"This is what I think happened. He provoked Puncheon's curiosity, probably with a photograph of some impressive-looking picture. He told Puncheon the same story he told me, about a shady dealer named Thompson who didn't want to be seen in public because the police were watching him. He played up the picture until Puncheon's mouth was watering for for the bargain. Then he gave Puncheon a message from Thompson asking him to meet him in the castle ruins, just as he did with me.

"Then he got on to the gang of skinheads. He must have found one of them who would be willing to kill a man if he was paid enough for the job. And I know how the kid did it, too. You gave me the idea when you told me how William does his poaching. A—what'd you call it?—a catapult. That would shoot one of those steel balls with enough force to kill a man. And some of the boys work at the plant that makes those steel balls. If that gang would beat somebody up for twenty pounds, which is what Villiers paid them to work on me, I'm sure one of them would go a little further for, say, a hundred."

"Possibly."

"All right. End of Puncheon. Next, Villiers went to Mrs. Puncheon as a friend of the family and a fellow-collector and offered to buy the painting. When that didn't work, he had a much better idea. He offered to take the whole collection to Sotheby's for her. She was grateful, she just wanted to get rid of it. So off he went to London with the pictures, only he never showed this particular one to them. He brought it back with the other worthless ones and put it in the Altoncester sale. I think he then went to the

181

viewing the minute it opened. He had prepared a label saying the painting was a copy by somebody named Maxwell, and he made it look old enough and unobtrusive enough to be convincing. He stuck the label on the back of the panel. You see, if the label had been on when the auctioneers had the picture, they'd probably have removed it. Then he hung the painting in an inaccessible spot where it wouldn't easily be seen before the sale.

"I'm sure he expected to get it for next to nothing. Maybe he would have, too, if I hadn't been there. He bid up as far as he could, but either didn't have enough money to go on, or, more likely, was afraid that if he went too high it would look suspicious. Anyway, as soon as I had it, he tried to get it from me.

"He tried buying it. Then he tried offering me swaps. When that didn't work, he set the skinheads on me with instructions to grab the picture away from me, and to beat me up."

I snapped my fingers. Something else had just occurred to me.

"When that failed," I said, "he got me to come to his house hoping his wife would get me upstairs and into bed. She's that kind of woman. He must have figured that he could then blackmail the picture out of me. Luckily, it didn't work that way, but I must say it came close. I thought he looked funny when he came in. He was disappointed.

"Anyway, he had something else in reserve, a fake note from Thompson, and a couple of photos he'd taken of pictures. But when I wouldn't bite, and when I insisted that the painting must be a good one, he was forced into a corner. He decided to kill me."

"You said he was an arranger of things—"

"Yes. He got to the castle early and fixed up the planks so they'd fall. That way, he wouldn't actually be doing anything to me. You see the distinction? But when I escaped, he lost control of himself. He must have been scared blue. He could see that if I got away I'd bring charges against him. He must have figured that the whole story about Puncheon's death would come out, too. All he could think of was wiping me out and that gave everything away."

I drank some of Hatch's good whisky and leaned back. I was feeling unreal, as if I were floating an inch or so above the chair. Now that I'd told it all, the story had the strangeness of a dream. I looked at the glass-cased carriage clock on the mantlepiece and saw that it was one-thirty. An hour and a half! It was only an hour and a half ago that I had met Villiers at the castle. He had been alive and plotting then, and now he was thoroughly dead.

"It's hard to believe," I said, following that idea.

"But it's logical," said Hatch, still thinking of what I had told him. "It all holds together. However, I can see why you don't want to tell the police. There's no proof of anything, as you said."

"No. I'll tell you something else," I said. "Something I just thought of. I know why there were pieces of glass all over the place when you found Puncheon's body."

"Why?"

"Tonight, after the planks collapsed, I started looking for Villiers. I saw him and went towards him, and suddenly discovered that I was looking at his reflection."

Hatch put down his glass. "How do you mean, his reflection?"

"The workmen keep some sheets of glass in a shed in the center of the courtyard. Well, the moon was bright tonight, and with the darkness of the shed behind it the glass was like a mirror. The night Puncheon was killed, there was a moon, too. Somebody told me that. The guy who shot at him probably stood on the wall or the gate towers, and mistook Puncheon's reflection for the man himself. I suppose if we went over there and studied the position, where Puncheon was standing, and what could have been between him and whoever was watching, we'd be able to tell just where the murderer stood. So the first shot shattered the glass. Puncheon must have turned to look at the noise and the murderer saw him, realized his mistake, and had a second shot."

"Very ingenious," Hatch murmured.

"I think so. Of course," I added, "there's another possibility."

"Another?"

I laughed. "A friend of mine here keeps telling me to look for alternatives. I just thought of one. That man William."

"Bullock? How does he come into it?"

"He's got a deep attachment to Sir Donald Sterlet, hasn't he?"

"I imagine one could say so. We are all villagers together. There is a sort of loyalty which binds us."

"Just so. If Puncheon had gone on with his plans for turning Pellet Lane into a quarry, Sterlet would have been out on his ass. William strikes me as being as hard as the local stone. He's accustomed to breaking the law, too. I can see him cold-bloodedly deciding to knock Puncheon off, the way he'd knock over a rabbit. Sterlet told me William was at the castle the night of the murder. All right, why couldn't it have gone this way:

"Villiers didn't bring in the skinheads. Instead, he decided to use that same trick he used for me, shoving the plank bridge right to the edge of the gap and expecting Puncheon to step on it and fall to his death. But William was there. He didn't know anything about that plan. He just saw Puncheon and decided to make use of the opportunity. He took out his slingshot, and pow!"

"No," said the Colonel, emphatically. "There I think you're wrong. Whatever you may think about William he hasn't the mentality of a killer. He may be hard, as you say, and loyal and tenacious. But a man-killer—? Never. Get that out of your head."

I chuckled. "Okay, if you say so. It wouldn't matter to me, Colonel. I'd never turn him in to the cops even if I'd seen him do the murder. Why should I? I've got a sense of loyalty too, even if I am an outsider."

I finished my whisky. "In any case," I said, "I don't imagine a little slingshot designed just for rabbits would have enough force to kill a man. I'd have thought it took something a little more accurate—a little more—"

My voice died away. My breath seemed to stop.

My eye had fallen on one of the trophies of arms. Hanging among swords, a pistol on each side of it, was the crossbow with the inlaid stock. It was the type called a prodd, designed for shooting birds, and indeed the man in my Dutch painting was shooting at a crow with just such a weapon: it had a double string with a pocket from which, instead of an arrow, a metal bullet could be shot.

I sat stupefied, unable to go on. Hatch's voice came distantly to me.

"Something like that?" he said.

I remembered something odd. The Colonel had told me that he'd heard the skinheads' car drive up to the castle the night of Puncheon's death. But according to Sterlet, William had been there and had heard nothing.

I wondered, however, whether he had *seen* anything.

If, for instance, he had seen Colonel Hatch shoot Puncheon with the crossbow wouldn't he have kept his mouth shut about it?

The Colonel, I knew, was a man who didn't mind taking chances. He had been a ruthless soldier. Suppose Puncheon hadn't phoned that night, as Hatch said, but had come to Hatch's house first? After making his offer for the Turner painting, he had gone on to the castle and Hatch, seeing the car headlights stop there, had followed with the crossbow, just on the chance.

He might have felt he had reason to destroy Puncheon for what he had done and was about to do to the village Hatch loved. But there was a deeper reason—hadn't that newspaperman told me that many people felt Mrs. Hatch's death was Puncheon's fault? The Colonel didn't show what was in his mind, and what was in his mind might have been the desire for revenge.

I focused my eyes again on the crossbow. And now I

could see that the double string was clean and new.

He must have practiced with it. He must have waited a long time for just such a chance. He had gone after Puncheon and shot at his shadow in the glass and then hit him with the second ball. All Villiers would have known was that somebody else had done his work for him. And if he had had any surmises he'd have kept them to himself, for after all whoever had done it had seen him there as well.

I dragged my gaze away from the crossbow and looked at Hatch. He was sitting bolt upright in his chair, regarding me fixedly with an expression I couldn't read. It was like that look you see on the faces of caged hawks in an aviary.

I liked him and admired him. And I owed him something. But beyond that I hadn't one single shred of proof that anything I guessed was true.

"No," I said, at last. "I don't think it can possibly have been anything like that."

He sighed, and his lips twitched in a smile. "Quite so," he said.

I awoke next morning knowing just what I was going to do. Without waiting to dress, I telephoned Jill's number.

As I had expected, Miss Trout answered. "It's Bob Eddison," I said. "Can you give me the address of the school where Jill teaches?"

"Why yes, of course," she replied. "But why not let her give it to you herself? I'll put her on."

Jill said, "Hello," in a forlorn voice

"You didn't go to school this morning."

"No. I wasn't feeling well."

"Jill," I said. "Listen, darling. Stay right there until I get there. I've got to talk to you."

"I don't think it will do any good," she replied, listlessly. "You said everything that needed to be said yesterday."

"Yesterday," I said, "I was an idiot. This is today. Please, Jill. Don't go out. I'll be there in an hour, maybe less. Okay?"

"Yes, all right."

I still wasn't sure she wouldn't run out on me. "I was nearly killed last night. I mean, really nearly killed."

"What do you mean? How?" She woke up at that.

"I'll tell you all about it when I see you. Wait for me."

I hung up and started to throw clothes on. I was shaving when the phone rang.

Mrs. Orchard said, "Sir Donald Sterlet is here to see you, sir."

"Sterlet? What for? Never mind," I said, "send him up."

I scraped off the last of the lather and, when he knocked, yelled, "Come on in." I stuck my head out of the bathroom and added, as he entered, "Take a seat. I'll be with you in a minute."

I came out shortly, buttoning my shirt. I was surprised to see that he was fairly neatly dressed in a tweed jacket, somewhat ragged at the cuffs, and a pair of whipcord slacks. Also, he appeared to be sober.

I said, "Sorry, I'm in a hurry. What can I do for you?"

"I've come to apologize," he said.

"That's all right."

"I behaved very rudely."

"It doesn't matter."

"It matters to me. I've seen William. He's told me about last night."

He was twiddling the end of his beard between thumb and forefinger, and scowling. I finished knotting my tie, and said, "You sound angry about it."

"I am angry. At myself, for being such a bloody fool. I thought you were a policeman of some kind."

"I guessed that. Well, you were wrong. So forget it."

"I was afraid, you see. Not for myself, but for—someone else. For William. I was afraid he might be mixed up in—in something."

I said, with careful deliberation, "I can assure you that he wasn't."

He said, with a surprised look, "How do you know what I'm talking about?"

"I know. I won't go into it. But if he told you what happened to me, then you won't be surprised if I tell you that Villiers had something to do with George Puncheon's death. And Villiers is dead. Nobody else is involved. Nobody's got anything else to say about the matter—including me."

"Christ! That's a bloody relief," he breathed. "I knew he'd been near the castle the night Puncheon was murdered. I found out he'd been using those steel ball-bearings

188

for his poaching. Shot them out of a catapult, if you know what that is. I was certain he'd done it.''

"Well, you can stop worrying.''

"Yes. It isn't just that, though,'' he went on. "I owe you something for what you did. You got me an income.''

"What are you talking about?''

"I don't know exactly what you said to my cousin Julia, but you must have persuaded her that I'm worth investing in. She came to see me and told me you'd said I had talent. She'd thought things over and decided to give me ten quid a week until, as she put it, I can stand on my own feet.''

"That's great,'' I said, and meant it.

He bent and picked up a brown paper parcel which had been leaning against the chair. "This is that thing of mine you liked,'' he said, handing it over. "It wasn't damaged when I threw it. I never was much good at sports. Would you like to have it?''

"Thanks a lot.''

"Don't reach for your wallet. It's a gift. And I'm going to make you another gift. I'll tell you about that painting you bought.''

"The Dutch landscape? What do you know about it?''

"What I don't know about it is who put the label on the back saying it was a copy by somebody or other. It isn't. It's by van Goyen.''

He had told me that once before but it hadn't registered because I had thought he was just throwing out names. But now that I thought about it, I could see why the painting had looked so familiar to me when I first saw it. Jan van Goyen died in 1656, and his small landscapes all have the same marvelous quality of light and space.

"I'm prepared to believe it,'' I said. "I had already guessed it was good, even before Villiers tried to kill me for it. And I presume you went with Puncheon and checked it for him when he bought it.''

He snickered. "More than that,'' he said. "I'm the one who flogged it to Georgie.''

189

"Flogged?"

"Sold it to him."

"I suppose I should have expected that. But my God, if it's really a van Goyen it could be worth five or six thousand pounds. How could you be so sure of what it was?"

"It had a signature and a date," he said, "but I painted them over."

I began to feel a premonitory queasiness. "Okay, just one more question," I said. "Where did you get it?"

"Oh, I stole it," Sterlet said, airily. "From the City Museum of—no, I don't think I'll tell you, but it's a small town in the North Country. It was easy to steal, too. Only one guard in the whole place. I just took it off the wall, popped it under my mac which I had over my arm, and walked slowly and calmly out."

"I see. But why?"

"I needed money, dear boy. I saw no reason a dead artist shouldn't support a living one. I told George it was good. He thought it was by Vermeer. He didn't have much sense, you know. Anyway, I got six hundred from him for it. Now you know what you've got."

He stroked his beard with a complacent grin. I fetched the painting and looked at it again, more attentively. Now, of course, I could see the slightly fresher patch where he'd covered the signature. He had done a good job, painting grass over it. A van Goyen! I could feel a certain smugness in the confirmation of my taste.

There was no reason why I shouldn't keep it. The museum had probably long since collected its insurance. The chances of anyone's recognizing it were almost nil—everybody in the trade knows how a reporter from the English magazine, *The Queen,* took a privately-owned signed Renoir drawing, which had recently been on exhibition, to a number of leading dealers asking for offers. Not one of them recognized it. A work by a relatively minor master like van Goyen, a small one from an obscure provincial museum, would join the hundreds of stolen paintings which slip in and out of dealers' hands every year without ever being known for what they are.

I was tempted all right. But not for very long. Puncheon had asked no questions about it: to him it was just a bargain which might turn out to be profitable. Villiers wouldn't have cared whether it was stolen or not. But I wasn't like them, and didn't intend to become like them. I remembered Simon saying, "The wise man owns beautiful things but he is not owned by them."

"I appreciate your telling me," I said to Sterlet. "I think, though, you'd better give me the name and address of the museum you took it from."

He gaped at me. "You must be mad," he said. "Are you planning to return it? What for? It's yours. You're a man with a feeling for paintings. Don't tell me you have scruples?"

"I'm afraid so, Not because I have any moral qualms. Just because I've seen what too much attachment to a piece of property can do to people. What was the museum?"

"No," he said. "Not on your life. Suppose they start asking awkward questions?"

"Don't be an idiot. All they can do is trace the picture back to Puncheon, and you and I are the only ones who know where he got it from."

He shook his head. "If you want to be an ass," he said, "I'm not going to help you." He grinned wickedly. "I'm going to see to it that you own a van Goyen whether you want to or not. I know how much the picture means to you."

Partly, no doubt, it was sheer perversity. But maybe part of it was that he really felt indebted to me. I put down my irritation.

"Okay," I said. "Never mind. I'll find out sooner or later. I'm going to be around for a while."

"Oh, really? I thought you were leaving for home shortly." He sounded disappointed.

"Did you? And you hoped, no doubt, I'd take this

191

embarrassing painting far away. Sorry. I'm staying. You see," I said, putting on my jacket, "I've got a girl here. I want to marry her but I can't get her to leave England. Well, you know, we're all so hidebound by certain ways of thinking that we take them as unalterable. Women are always supposed to follow their men—'Whither thou goest,' and so on. There *is* another alternative. I'm staying here with her."

He gave a soundless whistle. "You Americans are sentimentalists," he said. "I'd never do it, not for any woman. What about your job?"

"I can buy for my partner and our American customers over here and on the Continent. And there's nothing to stop me flying over to keep in touch. Anyhow, it doesn't have to be forever."

I looked at my watch. "Come on," I said. "I've got to get going."

He followed me to the door. "Well, if you think you can manage living in this bloody country," he said, "maybe we can have a drink together now and then."

"Put it this way," I said, as we started down the stairs. "You white faces came over and took my country away from me a few hundred years ago. Now I'll see whether I can't do the same for you."

I ran on ahead without waiting for him. I had already kept Jill waiting far too long.